William Young

The Rajah

An Original Comedy in Four Acts

William Young

The Rajah
An Original Comedy in Four Acts

ISBN/EAN: 9783337127527

Printed in Europe, USA, Canada, Australia, Japan

Cover: Foto ©Andreas Hilbeck / pixelio.de

More available books at **www.hansebooks.com**

THE RAJAH

An Original Comedy in Four Acts

BY

WILLIAM YOUNG

AUTHOR OF "PENDRAGON," "GANELON," THE DRAMATIC
VERSION OF "BEN HUR," ETC.

*As presented for two hundred and fifty consecutive nights,
at the Madison Square Theatre, New York,*

———

NEW YORK	LONDON
SAMUEL FRENCH	SAMUEL FRENCH, LTD.
PUBLISHER	PUBLISHERS
24 WEST 22D STREET	89 STRAND

THE RAJAH.

CHARACTERS.

HAROLD WYNCOT. Captain, in the East Indian service. Known to his associates as "The Rajah."

JOSEPH JEKYLL. Attorney. Agent in charge of the Wyncot estate.

MR. JOB. Churchwarden. Jekyll's associate in the trust.

RICHARD JOCELYN. Jekyll's clerk.

"BUTTONS." An omnivorous boy-of-all-work.

CRAGIN. Leader of strikers, in the Wyncot mines.

SYKES. A disgruntled miner.

JAMES. A footman.

GLADYS WYNCOT. Adopted daughter of the former proprietor of Wyncot Lodge, and its appurtenances, and ward of "The Rajah."

EMILIA JEKYLL. Daughter of Joseph Jekyll. Gladys' "one-and-only" friend.

MRS. PRINGLE. Housekeeper at Wyncot Lodge, and mother of "Buttons."

A groom. Miners in the Wyncot employ.

SCENE.—In and about Wyncot Lodge, an English country house.

TIME.—The present.

THE RAJAH.

ACT I.

SCENE.—*Exterior of Wyncot Lodge. Porch, and principal entrance, approached by steps,* R. 2. *A wing of building extending to* C., *on line with* 3. *Conservatory,* L. *Between house and conservatory, on line with* 3, *a high, ivy-mantled wall. Gateway, with gates of iron open-work, ornamental, in wall,* L. C. *Rustic table, and chairs,* R. C. *High-backed rustic seat,* L. C. *Path, leading off through ornamental shrubbery,* L. 1. *Branches of great trees, projecting from* R. *and* L., *overhead, making foliage-border. Park, at back, seen through gates, with glimpse of sea, in distance.*

(JEKYLL *and* JOB, *discovered, outside gates;* JEKYLL *ringing gate-bell, violently. Enter, through gates,* JEKYLL *and* JOB—JEKYLL *preceding.*)

JEKYLL. Walk in, Mr. Job! Walk in, sir! No one at 'ome? I assume the responsibility. (*looking about him*) Well, sir!—well, sir! 'Ere we are.

(*Enter* BUTTONS, *from house. He is eating a pasty, which he conceals behind him.*)

Ah! And 'ere *you* are. Well, sir, did you 'ear the gate-bell?
BUTTONS. (*with effort—his mouth full*) Yessir.
JEKYLL. You did? And w'y didn't you answer it? Where's your missus?
BUTTONS. In the 'ouse.
JEKYLL. "In the 'ouse." And the party that was expected—'as he arrived?
BUTTONS. (*negatively, with shake of the head*) Uh! uh!
JEKYLL. 'E 'asn't. We are first on the ground, Mr. Job. So much the better! (*to* BUTTONS) And now, sir!—come 'ere, sir! Do you know me?

3

BUTTONS. (*affirmatively*) Uh-huh!

JEKYLL. You do. And why don't you speak up? Wot 'ave you got in your mouth?

BUTTONS. Nothin', sir.

JEKYLL. " Nothin' "? Face about, you young vagabone! (*turns* BUTTONS *around, and takes the pasty*) W'y, wot's this? Bless me! Eh, Mr. Job?

JOB. (*sniffing at the pasty*) It's a pie, sir.

JEKYLL. (*in turn, sniffing at it*) A 'am pie!

JOB. Wot's left of it.

JEKYLL. (*to* BUTTONS) Eating—on dooty! 'Ow dare you?

BUTTONS. I likes to eat.

JEKYLL. 'E " likes to eat." 'Ere you 'ave it, Mr. Job—a lesson in political heconomy. W'y are the poor *halways* poor?—They " likes to eat." (*he takes* BUTTONS *by the ear*) And now, young man, do you know, sir, it's my opinion that this is a stolen harticle.

BUTTONS. (*protesting, vehemently*) S'elp me——

JEKYLL. That's wot it is, sir. And do you go in, and say to your missus that Mr. Jekyll is 'ere. Do you 'ear, sir?

BUTTONS. Yessir.

JEKYLL. Mr. Jekyll, *hand* Mr. Job. That they 'ave come on business, to meet Mr. Wyncot——

BUTTONS. (*squirming*) Yessir.

JEKYLL. And you may add that they advise 'er to give you a jolly good birching, and 'ereafter to 'ang the key of the pantry very 'igh. Well, sir,—do you 'ear?

BUTTONS. (*disengaging himself*) Yessir.

(*With sudden movement, he seizes the pasty, and retreats rapidly toward house.*)

JEKYLL. (*surprised, and slightly disconcerted, by* BUTTONS' *seizure of the pasty*) Eh? Get hout!

(*Exit,* BUTTONS, *into house.*)

Well, Sir! Well, sir! Sit down, Mr. Job.

(*They sit on rustic seat,* L. C. JEKYLL, *removing his hat, mops his forehead, with large, red, silk handkerchief.*)

I must say, I'm fairly blowed. Flesh is grass, Mr. Job. Flesh is grass.

JOB. (*with doleful unction*) "And is cut down, and withereth."

JEKYLL. Honly to reflect, that 'ere, but three short months ago—'ere we sat, with 'im that was, but is no more. Gone, Mr. Job! Vanished!

JOB. "Like a hexalation of the morning."

JEKYLL. A good man, sir!

JOB. A good man! And a hable man!

JEKYLL. Um! Well—'ardly that.

JOB. 'Ow, sir? Begging your pardon——

JEKYLL. Hover-rated—like all 'is class. Now, if by 'is own exertions 'e 'ad risen to such heminence!—as others, I think I may say, 'ave risen.—Not many, per'aps, but a few.

JOB. Ah! For example—your honorable self, sir!

JEKYLL. Eh? Thankee! But let that pass. 'Tis true, Joseph Jekyll 'as 'ad 'is struggles—if you choose to allude to 'im——

JOB. (*rolling his eyes, commiseratingly*) Ay, truly, sir!

JEKYLL. Wotever 'e 'as achieved, 'e freely owns 'is beginnings were 'umble.

JOB. 'Umble, and lowly!

JEKYLL. 'Ave I ever denied it?

JOB. As one might say, "the lowliest o' the low! "

JEKYLL. Um! Well—'ardly that. 'Owever, to resoom —speaking of the deceased:—'Ow does 'e come by 'is position? And wot does 'e do, to acquire all this? (*with wave of hand, indicating the surroundings*) 'Is 'ouses! —and 'is lands!—and the mines beneath 'em!

JOB. "The earth, and the fulness thereof! "

JEKYLL. Hexactly! The fulness, in this case, being coals—millions of tons of 'em, ready for the diggin'!— and 'ere at tide-water, ready for the shippin'! W'y, sir, 'e is simply *born*.

JOB. Dear! dear!

JEKYLL. 'E in'erits 'em—as who couldn't? And at the most critical period of 'is 'ole existence wot does 'e do? W'y, sir, 'e simply *dies*.

JOB. As who couldn't? True enough—as you say, sir!

JEKYLL. 'E dies. And mark wot follows:—Lacking a son, 'e selects, sir, as 'is heir, from among 'is forty nevews, the *honly* one whom 'e 'as never seen, and of whom 'e 'as 'eard but little—and that little, *bad!*

JOB. Oh, the perwerseness of the 'uman 'cart!

JEKYLL. Moreover—'e leaves a daughter. A daughter, as I say, though honly by adoption—and 'andsomely, too, 'e portions 'er off. But w'en he looks about 'im for a guardian, to protect 'er interests, on whom does 'e fix 'is eye? W'y, again on the nevew, aforesaid.

(Job *throws up his hands, in shocked acknowledgment of the impropriety.* JEKYLL, *rising, continues, with virtuous indignation.*)

Of all men, sir, 'e singles out '*im*—a military man, in a regiment of 'eathen—barbarian 'eathen—taking 'is ease under 'is punky, somew'ere in darkest Hindia, so to speak—*h*unmarried, and, from all accounts, gifted with most of the pecooliar failings of that 'ighly immoral clime!—'e singles out '*im*, and 'e appoints 'im, sir, to 'ave the care and the bringin'-up of a hinnocent and bloomin' girl, of scarce twenty summers!

JOB. (*rising*) 'Tis shocking, sir! 'Tis fairly un-Christian!

JEKYLL. A "hable" man, did you say, Mr. Job?

JOB. Figgeratively speaking, sir! Figgeratively! But surely, sir, 'tis not to be forgotten that 'e left you as agent in charge.

JEKYLL. (*mollified*) Ah! Thank'ee, Mr. Job! And *you*, as my hassociate! (*offering his hand*)

JOB. (*effusively, shaking* JEKYLL's *hand*) Thank'ee, Mr. Jekyll!

JEKYLL. 'Tis the one proof 'e 'as given of intelligence. And 'eavy will our burden be. From 'im that is to come we can expect *no* hassistance—and I shall tolerate *no* hinterference. (*taking MS. from his pocket*) I 'ave prepared 'ere, Mr. Job, a short effusion—as it were; a brief address of welcome. And you will observe, sir, that I 'ave seen fit to begin with wot you might call a 'igh 'and.

(*Enter, from house,* MRS. PRINGLE, *leading* BUTTONS, *who snivels, and draws his sleeve across his eyes.* JEKYLL, *unobservant of the intrusion, continues.*)

A 'igh, and a firm 'and, Mr. Job, if you would 'old the reins of office! But you shall 'ear. (*reads from MS.*) "Honored Sir "——

MRS. P. (*interrupting*) Which I 'opes, sir, that I speaks to Mr. Jekyll——

JEKYLL. (*looking up*) Ma'am!

MRS. P. And a man of station, and a keeper and attorney of the peace, as 'e is always named—though by some not hover-considered. (*turning to* JOB) And likewise to Mr. Job, for long years a church-warden in this westry, and a kindly man, as well I know 'im.—And 'is sister, which well I remember, being bed-fast, of a 'urt in the groin, from Hapril till Christmas-time—and with never a 'elper but these two 'ands——

JEKYLL. Woman!—don't hinterrupt. (reads) " Honored sir "——

MRS. P. But of all the tales, as I must say, which I 'ave this day 'eard!—For two, of such like, to combine against a hinfant—and 'im being weakly, and stunted in 'is growth, by reason of a lack of happetite—and that sweet-tempered, which I'm sure——

JEKYLL. Blow the hinfant! What does the vituperous female want? (attempts to lead JOB off, L.)

MRS. P. (following) And that sweet-tempered, which I'm sure—and lackin' the hinstinct to defend 'isself—being 'armless as a hangel—and likewise a 'alf-orphan——

JEKYLL. God bless me!

MRS. P. And 'ow, sir, you could lift a 'and, to nag 'im, and worrit, and depress 'im——

JEKYLL. Woman! Hobserve me! If you allude to the fact that I took young 'opeful by the ear, I'll explain, ma'am—and much good may it do you! I detected 'im in the act of eating a pasty—a pasty, ma'am, which 'e 'ad evidently filched——

MRS. P. " Filched," sir?

JEKYLL. Hexactly so! And I'm blessed if I 'ad it to do again, if I wouldn't wring 'is neck.

MRS. P. " Filched," sir— did I 'ear you say?

JEKYLL. Bless my 'eart!

MRS. P. Buttons—accused o' filchin'—and that before 'is wery two eyes! O, Lor'!— (turning to BUTTONS, and extending her arms) Buttons!

BUTTONS. (rushing into her embrace) Mamma!

(Enter, from the house, GLADYS.)

JEKYLL. Ha! Good morning, miss! Your servant, miss!

GLADYS. Mr. Jekyll! Mr. Job! Mrs. Pringle, the breakfast-room must be put in 'order immediately.

JEKYLL. Thank 'eaven!

(BUTTONS, retreating up R., draws the pasty from his pocket, and smells at it cautiously, picking out a morsel at intervals.)

GLADYS. (to JEKYLL and JOB) You know, of course, that Mr. Wyncot has not yet arrived.

JEKYLL. Ah, so we 'ave 'eard, miss.

GLADYS. But we expect him at any moment. You will, perhaps, walk into the house.

JEKYLL. Ah, thank'ee, miss! But I think we shall prefer the summer-'ouse. We 'ave a few notes to make, and the weather being so hoppressive——

GLADYS. Oh, certainly, as you like.

JEKYLL. Our compliments, miss; and we shall be on 'and, when needed. Come, Mr. Job, sir!—come, sir! Truly a 'appy escape!

(*Exeunt*, JEKYLL, *and* JOB, L. 1 E.)

GLADYS. And now, Mrs. Pringle, please don't answer, but go at once. Tell the cook to prepare nothing till he comes. But if you can think of anything that he is likely to fancy——

MRS. P. Which I'm sure, miss, being from Hinjy, which they are said to be werry fond o' peppers.

GLADYS. Oh, yes, I think you may put on the peppers. That will do.

MRS. P. Which it shall, miss. (*turning to go, she faces* BUTTONS, *who is picking at his pie*) Buttons!

(*With a quick movement, he puts the pie behind him, and leans toward her.*)

Bless the child! (*taking him by the hand, she leads him into the house, the pie still held behind him, being visible as he goes*)

(*Enter, through gate*, EMILIA.)

EMILIA. Gladys!

GLADYS. Emilia. (*they embrace*) Really, I thought you were never coming.

EMILIA. And I thought I should never get here. But you have seen him?

GLADYS. No!

EMILIA. Not yet?

GLADYS. I was up at four.

(*Impressively—seating herself on settee*, L. C. EMILIA *sits beside her.*)

The train was due at six. And it is now ten.

EMILIA. Oh, don't you almost hope that there has been a railway accident?

GLADYS. Well, I almost do.

EMILIA. And I should, outright. Do you know, I think it is just simply awful—that you should be compelled to live here, with such a man! And a total stranger!

GLADYS. Don't let us speak of him.

EMILIA. Then, too, if he were only older!

GLADYS. Well, he is not so *very* young—or, so they say.

EMILIA. Every man is young, Gladys, till he has been married—or thinks so. And we know that he is a brute. Or, why shouldn't he have come sooner? He was only in India. Yet here it is three months since his uncle died. And has he shown his face?

GLADYS. But you know he was very far inland—at Jemla—or somewhere; and perhaps they haven't the conveyances.

EMILIA. Don't try to excuse him, Gladys. And, of course he has all sorts of horrid habits. He smokes, certainly—and drinks—that we have been told.

GLADYS. (*with shudder*) Oh!——

EMILIA. And he will watch you like a hawk—that you may depend on.

GLADYS. Do you believe it, Emilia?

EMILIA. Whenever you go anywhere, you will have to ask permission. And if you buy so much as a corset-lacing, he will expect to know the price.

GLADYS. (*horrified*) Emilia!

EMILIA. Then he will probably want you to sing to him, and play for him, and mix his toddy——

GLADYS. I'll die first.

EMILIA. You don't know, Gladys.—And perhaps to fetch his dressing-gown and slippers, and button his boots.

GLADYS. (*rising*) Emilia, if you say another word, I shall think that you have come only to make me more miserable. As though I were not already miserable enough! (*turns away—hides her face*)

(EMILIA, *rising quickly, goes to her.*)

EMILIA. Oh, Gladys! (*embracing her*) Do you know? I have an idea. You shall come and live with *us*.

GLADYS. (*looking up*) With *you?*

EMILIA. Yes. With Richard and me—when we are married, of course.

GLADYS. Oh!

EMILIA. Well, you needn't say it in such a tone. I'm

sure, it is not among the impossibilities. Richard and papa are getting on very well together. Richard does all the inside work—that is, the office work—and papa, the outside work.

GLADYS.   Ah! the talking.

EMILIA.   Yes. It's something like that. And Richard says that as soon as he has made himself indispensable, he is going to demand a partnership. And then—Oh, dear!

GLADYS.   Emilia, you are not happy.

EMILIA.   No, I'm not. Papa has such a way about him. And Richard—though he is afraid of nothing else —yet when he comes face to face with papa, it does seem——

GLADYS.   Yes, I've noticed.

EMILIA.   It does seem as though there is a weakness in his legs. And his language, which is usually so beautiful, tangles up that dreadfully—Oh!

(*Enter, rapidly,* RICHARD JOCELYN, *through gate. The girls separate, and gaze at each other.* RICHARD *pauses, inside the gate, and strikes an attitude.*)

GLADYS.   Emilia, you expected him.

EMILIA.   Gladys, I'm surprised that you can think so.

RICHARD.   Emilia!

EMILIA.   Richard! (*she runs into his arms*)

RICHARD.   (*embracing her*)   Ah!—You won't mind, Miss Wyncot?

GLADYS.   Oh, dear, no! But I should have told you, Emilia—your papa is here.

EMILIA.   Papa!

RICHARD.   (*instantly releasing her, with tragic consternation and despair*)   " 'Twas ever thus! " " Papa! "

GLADYS.   He is in the summer-house, with Mr. Job. But you can keep a lookout, you know.

(*Exit,* GLADYS, *into house.*)

RICHARD.   Ah! thank you! The summer-house! Is the summer-house visible from this spot? (*looks off,* L. 1 E.) It is not. It is then to be inferred that this spot is not visible from the summer-house. Emilia—once more!

(*They embrace.*)

EMILIA.   O, Richard!

RICHARD.   I saw you crossing the paddock, Emilia, and

I followed. I fancied, Emilia, I fondly fancied, that for one brief moment, I might enjoy the blissful opportunity of meeting you, at a convenient and respectful distance from the exceedingly numerous individual whom you call "Papa." But 'twas not to be.

EMILIA. O, Richard!

RICHARD. It is not simply that he is numerous, Emilia. He casts a shadow, as it were. Even here, I am sensible of a diminution in the heat of the sunshine. They call it a warm day, Emilia—and so I thought it. But I begin to find it cool. Brrr!

EMILIA. Richard, you are afraid of papa.

RICHARD. Preposterous, Emilia!

EMILIA. You are. And what is worse, you let him know it. Now, that is not the way to get along with papa. Papa is a very good man—at heart. But he wants to be bullied.

RICHARD. Ah! He wants it. But does he wish it, Emilia? For therein lies a distinction.

EMILIA. And how, then, do you ever propose to ask him?

RICHARD. How, indeed? Emilia, it is a question—a question which I have pondered long and painfully. At times I have thought that it might be best to address him a letter—from a locality neither too near, nor yet too far.—Say, China.

EMILIA. Richard!——

RICHARD. And then again I have thought that the next county might answer.

EMILIA. Richard, listen to me! This must cease!

RICHARD. I fear it, Emilia.

EMILIA. Hereafter, you will assert your rights, and treat papa as he deserves.

RICHARD. Emilia, you would not have me strike him?

EMILIA. "Strike him?" Nor for the world!

RICHARD. Thank you! For your sake, I will not.

EMILIA. But when he speaks to you, you will answer him—respectfully—but firmly.

RICHARD. You advise it, Emilia?

EMILIA. You will give him to understand that you are not to be put down——

RICHARD. Ah!

EMILIA. Not to be put down! And, though at first he may not seem to like it——

RICHARD. No—I fancy——

EMILIA. And may even give you some little annoyance——

RICHARD. It is not improbable.

EMILIA. My word for it, he will soon become accustomed to the change, and admire you all the more.

RICHARD. But *I*, Emilia—do you think that *I* shall become accustomed—No matter! The advice is apropos.

EMILIA. And you will adopt it?

RICHARD. From this day forth—from this hour forth, it shall regulate my conduct. It chimes, Emilia, with a sentiment which I have long smothered. And now, that you become answerable for the consequences——

EMILIA. But you will do nothing rash?

RICHARD. Emilia, is not your image always with me? It shall plead for him, Emilia.

(*Enter,* L. 1 E., JEKYLL *and* JOB.)

Even in my wildest moments——

(*Stops, observing* JEKYLL, *who is glaring at him.*)

EMILIA. Richard!

RICHARD. Horror! Misery! Ruin!

EMILIA. (*in whisper of consternation*) Papa!

JEKYLL. Well, sir! Well, sir! Well, sir! Can I believe my heyes?

EMILIA. (*aside to* RICHARD) Say something! Say something—but be firm!

RICHARD. Oh! certainly!

JEKYLL. It was my himpression, sir, that I left you in charge of the hoffice.

EMILIA. Why, so you did, papa. (*aside to* RICHARD) Respectful, Richard, but firm!—Why, so you did, papa, but something has happened. What it is, Mr. Jocelyn will tell you. But it must be something important, for he has been looking for you everywhere.

RICHARD. Emilia!

JEKYLL. Oh! 'e 'as, 'as 'e?

EMILIA. Yes, and I have come to spend the day with Gladys; and so we met.—And—that is all. (*kissing* JEKYLL) Good-bye! (*runs into the house*)

RICHARD. " Alone!—Alone! "——

JEKYLL. (*regarding him fixedly over his spectacles*) Umph! Well, sir?

RICHARD. " Alone on a wide, wide sea! " Ha!—Mr. Jekyll——

JEKYLL. Hat your service! Well, sir?

RICHARD. The fact is——

JEKYLL. Ha! the fact is—— (*advancing*) Well, sir? The fact is, as I understand, something 'as 'appened.

RICHARD. Very true, sir! Or rather—if you will permit the correction in the pleadings—something is perhaps about to happen.

JEKYLL. Ha! as I imagine. Well, sir?

RICHARD. I have now been in your employ, Mr. Jekyll——

JEKYLL. Why, so you 'ave, sir—and still are.

RICHARD. Presumably. We will waive that point—with leave to except and amend.—But in relation to your daughter——

JEKYLL. 'Ow, sir? Hexcuse me! In relation to *wot?*

RICHARD. (*flurried*) As I have already remarked——

JEKYLL. As you 'ave, sir.

RICHARD. Or rather, was about to remark——

JEKYLL. One question:—By wot excuse do you connect my daughter with your hofficial duties?

RICHARD. Ah! As I was just proceeding to state——

JEKYLL. Well, sir?

RICHARD. Your daughter—when she informed you that the principal motive of my visit here was the desire of meeting you—H'm!

JEKYLL. Well, sir?

RICHARD. Well, sir, she was guilty——

JEKYLL. "Guilty?"

RICHARD. Of a slight misapprehension of the facts. For the truth is——

JEKYLL. Ho! We are getting at it.

RICHARD. We are, sir.—The truth is—— (*aside, with sudden and desperate determination*) And non-suit me, if it isn't!—The truth is, Mr. Joseph Jekyll, that of all my somewhat extensive acquaintance, both generally speaking, and at this present particular moment, you, sir, are the last—Mr. Joseph Jekyll!—or, as you yourself might more elegantly phrase it, the "hultimate hindividual," whom I have any desire to see. Good-morning! (*turns suddenly, puts on his hat. defiantly, and strides out through the gate*)

JEKYLL. Mr. Job!——

JOB.. Mr. Jekyll?

JEKYLL. Do you hobserve anything strange in my appearance, Mr. Job?

JOB. Why, no, sir. Not as I discover.

JEKYLL. Anything that could invite such a houtburst? This requires attention.

JOB. That it does, sir.

(*Trampling of horses, and the sound of wheels—without, at back, off L.*)

JEKYLL. But wot do I 'ear? 'Orses? He is 'ere.

(*shouting*) The 'ouse, there! The 'ouse! — Look lively!—James! Mrs. Pringle! Hemilia! Make 'aste, there!

(*Enter, from house,* JAMES, MRS. PRINGLE, *and* BUTTONS, *followed by* EMILIA.)

Make 'aste! Hemilia, where's Miss Wyncot?
EMILIA. Not coming.
JEKYLL. Not coming? Bless my 'eart!—James! The flag! 'Oist your bunting.
JAMES. Flag, sir?
JEKYLL. The master's at 'ome. Show your colors! Look lively!
JAMES. Yes, sir.

(*Exit,* JAMES, *into house.*)

JEKYLL. (*to* BUTTONS) 'Ere, Young 'Opeful! Stand you 'ere, sir! Mouth shut! Heyes open!

(*Stands* BUTTONS, R. C., *in grotesque attitude.*)

Mrs. Pringle, ma'am—I think this is about the proper hattitude for you.

(*Placing her,* R., *and regarding her critically.*)

MRS. P. Lor', sir!

(*Enter, back of gates, from* L., *a groom, who rings the gate-bell. Enter,* JAMES, *from house.*)

JEKYLL. (*to* JAMES) Hanswer the gate, sir!
JAMES. Yes, sir.

(JAMES *goes out through gate, and he and groom exeunt off* L. JEKYLL *goes* L., *leading* JOB *with him, strikes an attitude, and looks about him with satisfaction.*)

JEKYLL. Ah! Horder, now!
WYNCOT. (*without, at back, off* L.) Gently there, my good fellow!
JEKYLL. Horder!
WYNCOT. (*without—approaching*) James!—I presume you are called James—the umbrella!

(*He appears in gateway, looking back toward* JAMES, *who follows him, carrying umbrella, hat-box, and rug.* WYNCOT *is dressed in stylish, light, traveling suit, and walks, and speaks, languidly.*)

JAMES. (*appearing beside* WYNCOT) Yes, sir. (*he offers umbrella*)
WYNCOT. Spread it.

(JAMES *obeys;* WYNCOT *takes umbrella.*)

JEKYLL. (*aside to* JOB) Bless my 'eart!
WYNCOT. (*to* JAMES) Ah! Thank you!

(*He advances leisurely through gateway, sheltering himself with umbrella. Exit,* JAMES, *with luggage, into house.*

JEKYLL. (*when* WYNCOT *is fairly on—waving red handkerchief*) 'Ip!—'Ip!—'Ooray!
WYNCOT. (*with deprecatory gesture to* JEKYLL) Gentlemen, good-morning!
JEKYLL. Ha! Good-morning, sir! Your servant, sir! H'm!

(*Unrolling MS. .of address—begins to read.*)

" Honored sir "——
WYNCOT. (*interrupting*) Pardon me!

(*He turns to* EMILIA, *whom he has just observed, and removes his hat.*)

I presume I address Miss Wyncot.
EMILIA. No, sir! You do not.
WYNCOT. Ah! Then may I ask——
EMILIA. You may. I am Miss Jekyll, sir. And this is my father, Mr. Joseph Jekyll, the agent in charge of your estate.
WYNCOT. So?

(JEKYLL *bows profoundly.*)

EMILIA. And this is Mr. Job, his associate.
WYNCOT. Gentlemen! (*nodding*)
JOB. Devoted, sir, I'm sure.
EMILIA. And Miss Wyncot is indisposed, and for. the present begs to be excused.

Wyncot. Thanks! Quite a compendium. But, Miss—
Jekyll, will you do me a favor?

Emilia. A favor, sir?

Wyncot. The fact is, I have met with a most distressing accident.

Jekyll. Haccident, sir?

Wyncot. (waving Jekyll aside) My heavy luggage being a few hours behind, I had relied on my traveling-bag for change of apparel; but, somewhere on the road, my man took a fancy to abscond—poor devil!—I had compelled him to travel second-class—and the " Gladstone " apparently shared his disgust, and vanished with him.

Jekyll. (in boisterous appreciation of the joke) Haw! Haw! Capital! (nudging Jon) " Gladstone "—bag, you know. " Second-class "!

(Wyncot, turning, fixes his eye-glass, and gazes on Jekyll curiously and coldly. Jekyll loses his assurance, and adds obsequiously.)

Hexcuse me, sir!

Wyncot. (turning again to Emilia) You will explain to Miss Wyncot?—And make my excuses, for being compelled to appear before her, in my—present, somewhat disordered condition?

Emilia. (sarcastically) Oh, sir—with pleasure!

(Exit, into house.)

Wyncot. (to Emilia, as she vanishes) Thanks! You are very kind. (seating himself, R., turns to Jekyll) Now, you may go on.

Jekyll. Ha! Very good, sir! (reads) " Honored sir "——

Wyncot. (interrupting) One moment!

(Turns to Buttons.)

You, my lad—what are you called?

Buttons. Buttons, sir.

Mrs. P. (advancing) " Buttons! " O, Lor'! Which true it is, but 'is real name, sir—as 'is father would 'ave it—Hedward Adolphus——

Wyncot. (interrupting) Buttons!—come here!

Mrs. P. (leading the reluctant Buttons forward) Come, lovey!—My son, sir—and a growin' boy——

Wyncot. (giving Buttons the umbrella) Hold this.

Buttons. Yessir.

(*Taking umbrella, holds it carefully above himself— standing stolidly, face front.* WYNCOT *looks at* BUTTONS, *over his shoulder.*)

MRS. P. Bless 'im! (*rushing to* BUTTONS, *seizing him, and correcting his error*) Hover the gentleman—*to* be sure!

(BUTTONS, *pushed into position by* MRS. P., *holds the umbrella over* WYNCOT.—MRS. P., with *clasped hands, regards him with pride.*)

WYNCOT. Thanks! (*to* JEKYLL) Now, you may go on.
JEKYLL. (*mopping his brow—half aside, to* JOB) Well!—it is to be 'oped so. *H'm!*

(*Again, clearing his throat, assertively, reads, with oratorical emphasis:*—)

" Honored sir:—W'en, in the wise, but 'ow often hinscrutable dispensations of Providence, a man of means, and a man of mark, like to the late deceased—a man, moreover, of towering *hintellect*, and vast and gigantic *henterprise*—the prop and stay of a 'ole community—for such 'e was, and more—w'en such a man is brought low; and all 'is 'oldings and undertakings fall—as 'ow oft we see them do—into the 'ands of inexperience, and onto the 'ead of mediocrity, like a havalanche from a 'ousetop—it be'ooves——
WYNCOT. (*interrupting*) Ah!—once more! Pardon me, Mr.—— (*pausing, forgetful of the name*)
JEKYLL. · (*snappishly*)· Eh? *Jekyll*, sir.
WYNCOT. Jekyll—to be sure! Let me try to remember. But does this relate to business?
JEKYLL. To business? Well, hin a measure. Yes, sir.
WYNCOT. Ah! So I began to suspect. But surely, Mr. Jekyll, you can appreciate my condition. I have just completed a very exhausting journey. And you, I observe, are perspiring.
JEKYLL. (*mopping his forehead*) Well—who wouldn't, sir?
WYNCOT. Very true! Then, shall we say, to-morrow?
JEKYLL. " To-morrow," sir?
WYNCOT. For the remainder of the—— (*indicating* MS., in JEKYLL's *hand*)
JEKYLL. Haddress, sir?
WYNCOT. Exactly!—Or, the day after.—Or, when I send for you. That will be better.

2

JEKYLL. (*turning to* JOB) Bless my 'eart!

JOB. (*making ear-trumpet of his hand*) Eh?

WYNCOT. You won't mind the trouble of calling again? (*taking cigarette-case from his pocket*)

JEKYLL. (*sarcastically*) Ho, not at all, sir! Hon the contrary!—— (*to* JOB) Did you hever—— '.

WYNCOT. Thanks! Then we will consider it arranged. (*lighting cigarette*)

JEKYLL. Hat your service!

WYNCOT. You are very kind.

JEKYLL. (*with increased sarcasm*) And we wish you, sir, a 'appy recovery, from your most hextraordinary——

WYNCOT. (*interrupting*) Thanks! Good day!

JEKYLL. W'ere's my 'at?

(*Crossing and recrossing, excitedly, in search of his hat, which he has left on bench, L. Seizes hat, claps it on his head, and starts toward gate.*)

JOB. (*approaching* WYNCOT, *with genuflexion, hat in hand*) Most kindly, sir, I'm sure——

JEKYLL. (*colliding with* JOB, *and exploding*) Hout of the way, Mr. Job!

(*He strides rapidly out through gates, and exit, off L. Exit* JOB, *following* JEKYLL.)

WYNCOT. (*giving them a parting glance, exhales a long sigh of relief, and turns to* MRS. P.) Phew!—And now—ah——

MRS. P. (*coming quickly forward*) Pringle, sir. And to most, *Mrs.* Pringle—though from you I could 'ardly expect.—And for seven years 'ousekeeper 'ere, at this lodge——

WYNCOT. (*interrupting*) Just so. Your name is Pringle, and you are the housekeeper. You can tell me then if I can have a biscuit and a glass of sherry?

MRS. P. Ho, yes, sir! Which for two hours, sir, your breakfast 'as been ready in the breakfast-room. Though for that matter, as I must say, the wittles being yet uncooked——

WYNCOT. Ah!—and how far is it to the breakfast-room?

MRS. P. 'Ow far, sir? Well, sir, it 'as never been surweyed.

WYNCOT. Then, will you, Mrs. Pringle, survey it? Thank you! And, if not too far, expect me soon.

MRS. P. Which I 'opes, sir——

WYNCOT. Thank you! You may go.

MRS. P. Though I *will* be free to say, sir——

WYNCOT. Thank.you, Mrs. Pringle!

MRS. P. O, Lor'!

(*Exit*, MRS. P., *into house.*)

WYNCOT. (*after pause*) Buttons!

BUTTONS. (*feebly—maintaining his constrained position*) Yessir.

WYNCOT. I perceive that we are in the shade. And you seem fatigued.

BUTTONS. (*still more feebly*) Yessir.

WYNCOT. Lower the umbrella, and consider yourself excused.

BUTTONS. (*lowering umbrella—with sigh, in imitation of* WYNCOT'S) Phew!

(*Enter, at the same instant, from house,* GLADYS. *She pauses on the steps.*)

WYNCOT. (*observing her, and rising quickly*) Ah! At last! (*waving* BUTTONS *aside*) I have been once deceived; but this time, I trust—Miss Gladys.

GLADYS. (*frigidly*) Miss Wyncot, sir.

WYNCOT. (*bowing, apologetically*) To be sure! Quite right! But, pray be seated, Miss Wyncot. (*placing chair for her,* R.)

(GLADYS, *ignoring the proffered chair, crosses* L., *and seats herself on bench.* WYNCOT *gazes after her, quizzically.*)

Thanks! You are very kind. And again I am corrected. (*resuming his seat,* R.) But, really, Miss Wyncot, I—I am very pleased to meet you.

GLADYS. (*distantly*) Thank you, sir!

WYNCOT. Though it must be confessed the circumstances are—somewhat peculiar.

GLADYS. I appreciate that fact, sir.

WYNCOT. Ah—no doubt! And you will scarcely be surprised, Miss Wyncot, that——

(*Pauses, and looks over his shoulder at* BUTTONS, *who stands up* C., *leaning on umbrella, and listening intently.*)

BUTTONS. (*after pause*) Yessir?

WYNCOT. You may go.

(BUTTONS, *with umbrella, retreats hastily toward house. At steps, pauses, looks back, takes pasty from pocket, and biting into it, exits, into house.* WYNCOT *turns again to* GLADYS.)

You will scarcely be surprised that I exhibit but little grief for a relative whom I never had the pleasure of meeting, and whose obsequies were over before I received word of his death.

GLADYS. I am *not* surprised, sir.

WYNCOT. Ah!—thank you! And so, if you please, we will dismiss that phase of the subject.

(GLADYS *bows a sarcastic assent.*)

It is presumable, too, Miss Wyncot, that—you are aware of the provision, in my late uncle's will, which—makes me responsible for your welfare, and—conduct, and so forth—as guardian? (*speaking with hesitation, born of slight embarrassment*)

GLADYS. I am, sir—most painfully aware of it.

WYNCOT. Ah!—naturally, of course! And you are prepared, I trust, to make my—burden—pray pardon the word!—as light as possible?

GLADYS. (*emphatically*) I shall give you but very little trouble, sir.

WYNCOT. Ah—I am sure of it. Thank you—very much! And I have no doubt, Miss Wyncot, that, by-and-by, when we know each other better, we shall——

GLADYS. Well, sir? Respect each other more?

WYNCOT. Oh, by no means!—That is——

GLADYS. Because, if that is what you wish to say, I may as well tell you that, so far as one of us, at least, is concerned, your confidence is not well founded.

WYNCOT. Indeed?

GLADYS. And it is possible that my knowledge of you does not need to be extended.

WYNCOT. Really? You have heard of me, then?

GLADYS. (*looking away*) I wish that I never had.

WYNCOT. But India is very far away, Miss Wyncot.

GLADYS. There are means of communication.

WYNCOT. Ah! I begin to understand. You have a friend—who has met me abroad?

(GLADYS *again bows assent.*)

And he has furnished you with my character?

GLADYS. Yes!

THE RAJAH. 21

WYNCOT. In sober truth, Miss Wyncot, you begin to interest me. I should very much like to know in what esteem I am held by my old associates.

GLADYS. And you think it would please you?

WYNCOT. (*with shrug*) Well—I am not hard to please. Besides, you may have been misinformed, you know.

GLADYS. In which case, no doubt, you will set me right.

WYNCOT. With pleasure.

GLADYS. (*impatiently*) Oh!—And of course you will confess, if the information be true?

WYNCOT. I give you my word of honor.

GLADYS. I have half a mind to gratify you.

WYNCOT. I would, Miss Wyncot.

GLADYS. (*producing letter*) It is not likely that you remember the writer of this—since he, himself, says so——

WYNCOT. Ah! Documentary evidence!

GLADYS. Besides, I can easily make sure——

(*Holding the letter, as if about to tear it.*)

WYNCOT. Precisely! By tearing off the signature.

GLADYS. (*hesitating*) But I don't know if I should——

WYNCOT. Come! Doesn't it strike you as fair?

GLADYS. In any case, it is only proper to say that it was written by a person in whom I have entire confidence——

WYNCOT. It is to be hoped so.

GLADYS. And who was a very dear friend of my papa's —my *real* papa's. I knew that he had lived in India——

WYNCOT. Yes.

GLADYS. And when I heard of your appointment as my—— (*hesitates*)

WYNCOT. Guardian. Exactly! It *is* an awkward word.

GLADYS. Well, I naturally wished to know something about you——

WYNCOT. Proper enough.

GLADYS. And so, on the chance of his knowing you, I wrote to him.

WYNCOT. And this is the reply.

GLADYS. (*with sudden resolution, tears off signature, rises, crosses R., and hands letter to* WYNCOT) And this is the reply. (*she returns, L., and stands, as if ready for flight, watching* WYNCOT, *furtively*)

WYNCOT. (*half rising, as he takes the letter*) Thank

you! (*sinks back into chair*) Umph! (*reads*) "My dear Gladys"—Familiar—at least!

GLADYS. Oh, but he is elderly!

WYNCOT. Ah! that makes a difference. (*reads*) "My Dear Gladys:—During my sojourn in Bengal, I made the acquaintance of your lately appointed guardian, and remember him well, though he has probably forgotten me."—Humph! Probably! "Unless he has greatly changed, he is a good-enough sort of fellow,"—Come! that is not so bad.

GLADYS. O, you will find very little like that.

WYNCOT. Ah! In that case, I had best read it again: "He is a good-enough sort of fellow, but so unutterably indolent, that if the end of the world were to be announced, he would simply light a fresh cigarette—and possibly order a brandy and soda."

(GLADYS *gasps, and turns away her head.*)

Humph! It does not improve, as we progress.

GLADYS. Oh, read on!

WYNCOT. "While in the East, he occupied his time in the various mild forms of dissipation practiced by Europeans in that climate, and in making love, in a languid sort of way, to the officers' daughters, and—I regret to add,"— (*pauses—inspects sheet*) Ah, yes!—"wives."

GLADYS. Oh! And you don't deny it?

WYNCOT. Well!—he perhaps strains a point. I have no positive recollection of any occurrence of the kind. Still—I confess—my memory is treacherous. Let us read on:—"When not too lazy to assert an opinion, he was disposed to be autocratic; for which reason, and because of his indolence, above noted, and his love of luxury, he acquired the title of 'The Rajah,' which he wore with becoming indifference.—I sympathize with you, my dear Miss Gladys, in the trying situation, in which you are placed, but can see no remedy, unless the Court of Chancery could be induced to interfere. Sincerely," etc.

GLADYS. Well?

WYNCOT. Well!—he has apparently known me.

GLADYS. And you confess?——

WYNCOT. My dear Miss Wyncot, how can I do otherwise—having given you my word of honor?

GLADYS. (*retaking letter, with satirical bow*) Then, sir, while I admire your candor, I must ask you to excuse me, if I prefer to annoy you with but little of my society.

WYNCOT. And you are determined not to like me? (*rising*)

GLADYS. Can you ask that question?

WYNCOT. Well—yes—I presume I can ask it.

GLADYS. But you certainly expect no answer. And now I have but one thing more to say——

WYNCOT. But one?

GLADYS. And that in relation to your affairs.

WYNCOT. Ah! And you, too!—But proceed.

(He sinks back into chair.)

GLADYS. I think you should know, sir, that everything is not as it should be.

WYNCOT. Indeed?

GLADYS. For several weeks, there has been much dissatisfaction among the men. I know but little of the cause. But, led by a newcomer, whom Mr. Jekyll has employed, they have been holding meetings, and making threats.

WYNCOT. Is it possible?

GLADYS. It is the common report that at any hour an outbreak may occur, and I trust, sir, that you may sufficiently exert yourself, to preserve at least a portion of what your uncle has left you, from ruin. *(turns to go)*

WYNCOT. Ah—really!—But, stop!— *(rising)*

GLADYS. Good-day!

(Exit, GLADYS, into house.)

WYNCOT. What a peculiar girl! What a *very* peculiar girl! In some respects, a truly remarkable girl! Not beautiful, certainly!—And yet—— *(musingly, lighting a fresh cigarette)*

(Enter, quickly, through gates, from off R., CRAGIN, in miner's dress. He moves with aggressive, swinging strides, and is followed by SYKES, and half-a-dozen others, garbed like himself, who advance more diffidently. Just within gates, all but CRAGIN hesitate, halt and remove their caps. CRAGIN, when within a step or two of WYNCOT, also halts—but remains covered. WYNCOT, turning, observes CRAGIN.)

Hello!—And who may you be?

CRAGIN. *(advancing another step, insolently)* That you'll learn, sir——

WYNCOT. Ah?

CRAGIN. That you'll learn, sir, when you've cast your eye over this. *(offers paper)*

WYNCOT. More documents!

CRAGIN. Though, in short, sir, I don't mind telling you. I am generally spoken to as Cragin. And these are my mates. And this, sir, is a copy of our demands, which we 'ave the honor to present to you.

WYNCOT. "Demands!" Then it is not a petition?

CRAGIN. Well, sir, we've drawed up petitions 'eretofore, but they didn't seem to justify our wery waluable time. So we've altered the style.

WYNCOT. Just so! (taking the paper) And you are called Cragin? (looking at CRAGIN sharply)

CRAGIN. (suspiciously—with bravado) Well? So I said. W'y not?

WYNCOT. And you speak for the men in the Wyncot employ?

CRAGIN. Again, w'y not?

WYNCOT. "Why not," indeed?—if they choose to entrust their interests to a stranger.

CRAGIN. "A stranger!" Ha!—you've been getting tips.

WYNCOT. (referring to paper) And this, I am to understand, is a statement of certain grievances—of which they complain?

CRAGIN. (turning to men) Well, mates?

SYKES. (with effort at valor) Ay, sir!

MINERS. (all—more or less courageously) Ay!—Ay!

WYNCOT. Very good! But, Cragin—so called—since when has it been the fashion for the spokesman, on an occasion like this, to wear his cap?

CRAGIN. (slightly disconcerted) 'Is cap, sir?

WYNCOT. That was my inquiry.

CRAGIN. (folding his arms, and smiling, with reinforced insolence) Well, sir, in respect of that, too, we're thinkin' of changin' the style——

WYNCOT. Ah?

CRAGIN. Having figgered it out, and agreed—unanimous— (with backward, angry glance at his weak-kneed companions) Eh?—you bloomin' tykes!—that caps was made to wear.

WYNCOT. You are progressive—I see. But, I can't quite follow you; for there are times when caps—as well as hats—should be removed. And this, I take it, is one of them. Come!—merely as a concession to custom—oblige me! (mildly, with gesture, suggesting the removal of the cap)

CRAGIN. (amused by the audacity of the request) Wot, sir?

WYNCOT. (in tones low, but impressive) Take it off!

(CRAGIN, *gripping his cap, cocks it on his head, more defiantly, and again folds his arms.*)

CRAGIN. (*with grin*) Ha! Werry sorry, sir!
WYNCOT. (*with sudden movement, seizing the cap from* CRAGIN's *head, and hurling it to the ground*) So am I.
CRAGIN. (*in amazement, and rage*) Eh?

(*He clinches his fists, and draws back his arm, as if to strike.* WYNCOT *eyes him, calmly.* CRAGIN's *threatening attitude slowly relaxes.*)

WYNCOT. Thanks! (*turning to miners, and referring to paper*) And now, my lads, I will peruse this. And you shall hear from me. Good-morning!

(*He turns on his heel, and walks languidly toward house.* CRAGIN, *with recurrence of rage, springs after him.* WYNCOT *turns, facing him, and eyes him, as before.* CRAGIN *again halts, and recoils.*)

Picture.

CURTAIN.

ACT II.

SCENE.—*Drawing-room, Wyncot Lodge. Walls, paneled; with hangings of tapestry. Double door, c., at back. Broad window, opening to floor, R. U. E., oblique; with heavy curtains, looped apart, giving view of ornamental grounds. Door, L. 1. Door, R. 2. Grate, with fire, R. 1. Escritoire, with writing materials, up R. Table, L. C. High-backed chairs, divans, etc. Woodwork and all furniture and furnishings, dark in tone, but rich. Chandelier, unlighted.*

(*Enter, at curtain,* GLADYS, *followed by* MRS. PRINGLE, *door, R. 2.*)

MRS. P. Which first, miss, it's the gate-bell that rings; and "Buttons!" it is, and 'e goes.
GLADYS. (*endeavoring to interrupt*) Mrs. Pringle——
MRS. P. And next, miss, it's the bell of the liberary;

and "Buttons!" it is, and 'e goes. And next, miss, it's the 'ot water for shaving; and "Buttons!" it is, and 'e goes.

GLADYS. Mrs. Pringle——

MRS. P. And 'im that driven and plagued of 'is life, with 'is collar about 'is ears—and likewise stiff as a ramrod—bein' 'eretofore used but to turn-downs! Which I 'ave only to say, miss——

GLADYS. Once for all, Mrs. Pringle, as I have already told you, it is now Mr. Wyncot who commands at Wyncot Lodge—and to him you must make your complaints.

MRS. P. Which I 'ave only to say, miss, that if Buttons is to be hunder-footman, and likewise valley-de-sham, then w'y not the wages of a valley-de-sham? Or, leastwise——

(*Enter, door* c., BUTTONS, *in new livery, with high collar. He walks stiffly and constrainedly.*)

Lor'! do but look!

BUTTONS. (*stretching his neck, announces in a shouting tone*) Mister Jekyll——

MRS. P. Bless 'im!

BUTTONS. Hand Mr. Job!

GLADYS. (*hopelessly*) Oh, Buttons!

MRS. P. (*admiringly*) For all the world like the Squire's own plush, at a county ball!—Buttons!

BUTTONS. (*rushing into her embrace*) Mamma!

(*Enter, door* c., EMILIA. *She wears hat and light wrap.*)

GLADYS. (*running up to greet her*) Emilia! (*they embrace*)

EMILIA. (*calling back through door*) Come in, papa! (*to* GLADYS) I found them waiting in the hall-way—so I took the liberty.

(*Enter, door* c., JEKYLL *and* JOB; *their hats in their hands.* JOB *lingers in doorway.* MRS. P., *aside, presents* BUTTONS *with an apple, which he eyes gloatingly, and munches clandestinely.*)

GLADYS. (*greeting her guests*) Oh, Mr. Jekyll! Come in, Mr. Job! I must ask you to excuse all short-comings in the present management of this household. You have come to see Mr. Wyncot?

JEKYLL. We 'ave.

GLADYS. Be seated! Shall I not take your hats?

JEKYLL. (*loftily—declining*) Ah, thank'ee! But, we

are 'ere by request—special, I may say—— (*appealing to* JOB)

JOB. Quite special!

JEKYLL. Of the honorable party, aforesaid; and our time being somewhat precious, we 'ope we shall not be detained.

GLADYS. I will send for him, at once. Buttons! you will go to Mr. Wyncot's room, and say to him that Mr. Jekyll and Mr. Job are here——

JEKYLL. By *happointment*.

GLADYS. By appointment. You understand?

BUTTONS. (*sighing, and pocketing his apple*) Yes'm.

GLADYS. Well, then! Immediately!

MRS. P. (*wiping* BUTTONS' *face with her apron*) Wot next? Poor dear!

GLADYS. (*severely*) And you, Mrs. Pringle, may be excused.

MRS. P. Which I am, miss. And "Buttons" it is, and 'e goes.

(*Exeunt, simultaneously,* BUTTONS, L. 1, *and* MRS. P., R. 2.)

JEKYLL. " A hangel mother's tender cares,
      'Ow touching to be'old! "

GLADYS. (*piqued*) Really, Mr. Jekyll, you are disposed to be facetious.

JEKYLL. 'Ow's that, miss? Not guilty!

GLADYS. And you may well have a poor opinion of my discipline; but you will remember, I trust, that there has been a *change* in the control of affairs at the lodge——

JEKYLL. Ho! pray, don't mention it.

GLADYS. And some of the effects you may have experienced.

JEKYLL. Well—possibly—per'aps!

GLADYS. Then I need say no more. And you will excuse us, now?

JEKYLL. Hif we must.

GLADYS. Mr. Wyncot will certainly ·be here very soon.

EMILIA. Good-morning, papa!

JEKYLL. Morning!

(*Exeunt,* GLADYS *and* EMILIA, R, 2.)

And now, Mr. Job, in the language of the poet, " 'Ere we are, once more."

Job. In the tents of the Ishmaelite—so to speak.

Jekyll. But mark my observation!—mark it well, sir!
If, by my presence on this occasion, I 'ave consented to
'umor 'is ecccentricities—not to call them by a 'arsher
name—it is owing, Mr. Job, to but one cause. You
fathom me?

Job. W'y, sir, I trust——

Jekyll. For the respect in which I 'eld 'is uncle—
that worthy man——

Job. A worthy man, sir!

Jekyll. That *great* man, Mr. Job!

Job. A great man, sir!

Jekyll. Well, sir, for the respect in which I 'eld *'im,*
and still 'old 'is memory, I 'ave resolved, sir, as a matter of duty, to guide the nevew through 'is present
crisis.

Job. And very kind in you, sir!

Jekyll. Thankee! *But, sir, thereupon,* and *there-
after——* (*pausing, significantly*)

Job. As you say, sir——

Jekyll. (*spreading his arms*) He*x*cuse me! I say
no more.

(*Enter* Wyncot, *door,* l. 1. *He is in dressing gown and
slippers, and carries a folded document.*)

Wyncot. Ah, gentlemen! Good-morning!

(Jekyll *bows, stiffly.*)

Job. Honored—most 'ighly, sir—I'm sure.

Wyncot. I trust I have not kept you waiting.

Jekyll. (*consulting watch*) H'm! Well, sir, not to
speak of.

Wyncot. Ah! I am sorry. And I further regret, gentlemen, that at our last meeting, which was also our first,
I treated you, perhaps, with what may have seemed a
lack of consideration.

Jekyll. H'm! Well, sir—again, not to speak of.

Wyncot. Thank you! The fact is, I was very much
exhausted, at the time, and was not then fully aware
of the obligation under which you proposed to place me.

Jekyll. (*aside to* Job) 'E alters 'is tone.

Wyncot. I knew, of course, that you were the active
business agents in charge of the estate——

Jekyll. Ha, thank'ee, sir!

Wyncot. But I have since discovered, in addition,

that for some years previous to my late uncle's death, you frequently acted as his confidential advisers.

JEKYLL. Sir, we 'ad that honor.

WYNCOT. I have therefore sent for you, to beg the benefit of your experience, in the somewhat trying situation in which I am now placed.

JEKYLL. (aside to JOB) The weather 'as changed, Mr. Job.

WYNCOT. May I impose upon you to that extent?

JEKYLL. Sir, we shall hesteem it a duty.

WYNCOT. And I shall appreciate the kindness. You have been furnished, I presume, with a copy of the address issued by my employes?

JEKYLL. (taking paper from his pocket) We 'ave, sir.

WYNCOT. Then, if you please, we will lose no time. Mr. Job, pray be seated.

(WYNCOT sits L. of table, which stands L. C. JOB seats himself on edge of chair, R.)

Mr. Jekyll, I shall be pleased to hear you.

JEKYLL. Ha, sir! Very good!

(He takes position, C., across table from WYNCOT, and clears his throat, preparatory to beginning—the unfolded paper in his hand.)

WYNCOT. (offering cigarette-case) Will you join me?

(JEKYLL declines, with abhorrent gesture.)

Ah, of course! You could hardly speak and smoke. Mr. Job—— (extending the offer to that individual)

JOB. Thankee, kindly!—but they goes to my 'ead, sir.

WYNCOT. Too bad! (to JEKYLL—lighting cigarette) Pardon me!—you don't object, I trust?

JEKYLL. (with dignity) Hevery one to 'is taste, sir!

WYNCOT. I shall not interrupt again.

JEKYLL. H'm! As I 'ave said—very good. (displaying the paper, which he holds) You 'ave doubtless observed, sir, that 'erein there are distinctly hembodied two distinct demands. (he waves the paper before WYNCOT'S eyes)

WYNCOT. I have observed.

JEKYLL. The first, in point of horder, relates to the wages of the men. Hin glowing terms—and to the inexperienced calculated to deceive—it proceeds to set forth that the wages aforesaid are at present *h*insuffi-cient. You follow me?

WYNCOT. I do.

JEKYLL. Very good, sir! But, don't get a'ead! Hon this subject of the working man, don't think to get a'ead of Joseph Jekyll, hattorney. *Hexperience?* Well, possibly—per-aps! And this I tell you, sir—this I hexpressly state, as a fact, sir, in political economy—give a working-man pie, and 'e will immediately ask for pudding; give 'im pudding, and 'e will ask for sauce. And there 'e 'as you—See? Very good, sir! Well, sir!—where shall we draw the line? Draw it, sir, at pie. Draw the line at pie, (*striking the table*) and there you 'ave 'im. See?

WYNCOT. I *begin* to see, Mr. Jekyll. In other words——

JEKYLL. Hin other words: the demand for an increase of wages, you will *hunconditionally* refuse.

WYNCOT. Ah! That, at least, is plain.

JEKYLL. I 'ope so. Very good, sir. To resume. Let us inspect now the second stipulation. This, you will take notice, himposes the condition, that a certain Cragin, who is the 'ead and front of the strike, be appointed to the position of " Overman." Very good, sir! Now, who is Cragin? 'Eaven knows. He is a new 'and, He is not, so to speak, the best man for the place; but he is, so to speak, a most ugly customer to 'andle. Well, sir,—what then? Happoint 'im! That will satisfy '*im.*

WYNCOT. No doubt!

JEKYLL. That will satisfy '*im*—and 'e will satisfy the others. The men do not admire 'im, but they are afraid of 'im. And so, without hexpense, you will 'ave satisfied all. Again, sir—see?

WYNCOT. I think I do, Mr. Jekyll. And a very shrewd scheme it is.

JEKYLL. Ah!—thank'ee, sir!

WYNCOT. I perceive, Mr. Jekyll, that you are not without claims to the confidence which my late uncle reposed in you.

JEKYLL. Ho, sir, you overw'elm me. And now if you 'ave but a pen and paper 'andy——

WYNCOT. Ah! but stop! One moment, Mr. Jekyll! I have been here but a short time, as you know; and yet —in my way—I have made some slight examination into the condition of affairs. I have learned, at least, that the earnings of the property are large, and that the wages of the men are small.

JEKYLL. Well, not hexorbitant, per'aps.

WYNCOT. No, not exorbitant. Now, it may be, Mr. Jekyll, that a taste of pie does beget a taste for pudding; and that with pudding may arise a desire for sauce. I believe, Mr. Jekyll, that even you and I do occasionally take sauce with our pudding.

JEKYLL. Why, yes, sir! Yes! Hat times.

Wyncot. And though I am not a man of experience, and of political economy, know absolutely nothing, it is nevertheless my conviction—my firm conviction, Mr. Jekyll—that the employer who cannot live and thrive, and yet allow his employes an occasional nibble at the pie of prosperity, should assign to some one who can.

(JEKYLL, *amazed, turns to* JOB.)

JOB. (*anxiously, his hand to his ear*) Eh?

JEKYLL. (*turning again to* WYNCOT) Well, sir——

WYNCOT. Well, sir—in short—you will see that the wages are promptly increased, in accordance with the list which I herewith provide. (*extending folded paper, which* JEKYLL *takes, hesitatingly*)

JEKYLL. Do you mean it?

WYNCOT. I do.

JEKYLL. You hastound me.

WYNCOT. I am really very sorry.

JEKYLL. You hastound me. I can say no more.

WYNCOT. I will endeavor to excuse you.

JEKYLL. But, of course, you hassume——

WYNCOT. Oh, completely—the entire responsibility.

JEKYLL. Ha! Thank'ee, sir!

WYNCOT. And we may therefore regard this problem as dismissed.

JEKYLL. Quite as you please, sir! (*aside*) 'Old your breath, Mr. Job.

WYNCOT. And now concerning the other matter.

JEKYLL. Ah! Well, sir?

WYNCOT. I have also investigated—to a certain extent—the case of this "certain Cragin;" and I quite agree with you that he is a desperately ugly customer.

JEKYLL. Ho! In that we *do* agree?

WYNCOT. We do.

JEKYLL. And you recognize the policy of providing for 'im?

WYNCOT. (*rising*) Without delay. But, as "ugly customers" are desirable neither as overmen, nor undermen, you will see to it, Mr. Jekyll, that in *his* case the provision is one of discharge.

JEKYLL. "Discharge," sir?

WYNCOT. Discharge.

JEKYLL. Do I 'ear you?

WYNCOT. I trust you do. And so—that, also being settled—— (*offering his hand*)

JEKYLL. But I beg your pardon!—Discharge?—Crages?—I should say, Wagin—and hincrease——

WYNCOT. The wages. Precisely! You quite understand me.

JEKYLL. Then, in both respects, you habsolutely and diametrically——

WYNCOT. Oppose my opinion to that of experience? Rash, perhaps; but I have a fancy to try the experiment.

JEKYLL. Oh, bless my 'eart!

WYNCOT. Good-day, Mr. Jekyll!

(JEKYLL, *turning, seizes* JOB's *hat from the table—where both his and* JOB's *have been resting—and starts towards door, up* C.)

JOB. (*following* JEKYLL, *and clutching his coat-tail*) Eh? Mr. Jekyll——

JEKYLL. (*striking off* JOB's *hand*) 'Ands off, you old hidiot!

JOB. But excuse me!—My 'at, sir!

JEKYLL. Your wot? Eh?

(*Claps* JOB's *hat on his head, realizes the misfit, and dashes it to the floor.*)

Be 'anged to you! (*seizes his own hat, and rushes out door,* C.)

(JOB, *picking up his hat, rapidly follows* JEKYLL—*looking back toward* WYNCOT, *and smirking, and bowing, conciliatingly, as he goes.*)

WYNCOT. Good-day, Mr. Job! Good-day!

(*Exit* JOB, *door* C., *following* JEKYLL. *At the same instant, enter, door* R., GLADYS *and* EMILIA. WYNCOT *turns, and greets them.*)

Ah, ladies! Your most obedient! Walk in! We have quite finished. Very annoying—these little matters of business, but— Pray, be seated. You got my message, Miss Wyncot?

GLADYS. I have received it, sir—and am here.

(She seats herself, R.—EMILIA *stands beside her.)*

WYNCOT. Ah!—and it is very good of you! I very much regret, Miss Wyncot, to be compelled to assert my authority, at such an early date——

GLADYS. *(half rising)* "Authority?"

WYNCOT. Well—call it, if you prefer, my personal influence.

GLADYS. Oh, no, sir! *(sinking back in her chair)* Let us call it authority, then, by all means!

WYNCOT. As you like!

EMILIA. *(aside to her)* It is coming, Gladys.

WYNCOT. But it has come to my knowledge that you are in the habit of rambling, somewhat extensively, about the country-side, in company with your friend, Miss Jekyll; and that you occasionally make use of a path which leads to the shore and the wharves, by way of "The Glen." A very romantic walk, I am told—quite lonely, and unfrequented—and so, of course, all the more attractive. But I think it advisable, for the present, that you should avoid it.

GLADYS. Indeed?

WYNCOT. In fact, that you should confine your strolls to the immediate neighborhood of the house. It will hardly be necessary to trouble you with the reasons——

GLADYS. Really! It is sufficient for me to know that you "think it advisable."

WYNCOT. Well—I trust so.

GLADYS. *(rising)* But, let me understand! Is this intended as an order?

WYNCOT. An "order?" No! Oh, no! For in that case you would immediately disobey it—of course! Consider it a mere suggestion. And so, perhaps, we may regard it as arranged. We shall meet, I trust, at dinner?

(Bowing, turns, and moves toward door, L. 1.*)*

EMILIA. Gladys!

*(*GLADYS *averts her face.* EMILIA, *stepping forward, decisively, calls after the retreating* WYNCOT.*)*

Mr. Wyncot!

WYNCOT. *(at door,* L., *turning)* Miss Jekyll——

EMILIA. Are you not ashamed of yourself?

WYNCOT. Well—positively—I——

EMILIA. No! you are not. It would be difficult, I fancy, to make you blush.

3

WYNCOT. But, I trust you don't think of trying.

EMILIA. After having been in the house but twenty-four hours, to attempt to dictate, in such a ridiculous fashion! As though Gladys were not able to take care of herself! What do you know about young ladies?

WYNCOT. Very little! Very little, I assure you.

EMILIA. And yet, from your manner, one would think you were the father of fifteen or twenty.

WYNCOT. Oh, Miss Jekyll!

EMILIA. But it may as well be understood, first as last; and I speak for Gladys, who perfectly agrees with me, in everything that I say—tell him so, Gladys——

GLADYS. Yes—perfectly——

EMILIA. It may as well be understood that here-after you are to attend strictly to your own affairs——

WYNCOT. Ah?

EMILIA. And are not to regard Gladys as one of them. It is true, the law gives you some slight advantage—which you are probably mean enough to use——

(WYNCOT *makes deprecating gesture.*)

But, if you should, do you suppose for one brief moment, that with the advantage of all the laws in existence, you can compel a young lady to do what she doesn't wish to do?

WYNCOT. Oh, not for one moment!

EMILIA. No!

WYNCOT. Pray, don't so misjudge me.

EMILIA. Then, perhaps you will resign your ridiculous pretensions?

WYNCOT. It would seem the safer course.

EMILIA. And we shall all get along comfortably—if not pleasantly——

WYNCOT. Yes.

EMILIA. And much trouble will be avoided—on both sides.

WYNCOT. Yes.

EMILIA. And besides, sir, you will be spared much fatigue.

WYNCOT. Without doubt! Yes.

EMILIA. And——

WYNCOT. Yes.—Well?

EMILIA. Well? Why don't you say something?

WYNCOT. But, my dear Miss Jekyll, you have said it all. I can positively think of nothing to add.

EMILIA. Oh, but don't I wish that *I* were a ward of yours!

WYNCOT. Thank you!—You are very kind. But, one is quite sufficient. However—since I can do no more—— (*strikes bell, on table*) You must permit me, at least, to provide you with an escort.

(*Enter* BUTTONS, *door* C.)

Buttons! You see these young ladies?

BUTTONS. Yessir.

WYNCOT. They propose to go for a walk. You will follow them—wherever they may go——

BUTTONS. Yessir.

WYNCOT. Being careful not to lose them from your sight. And if anything alarming should occur, I think I may rely on you to give me notice.

BUTTONS. Yessir.

WYNCOT. You may go.

(*Exit* BUTTONS, *door* C.)

And now, once more! Till dinner!

(*Again bowing, exit, door,* L. 1.)

GLADYS. What shall be done with such a man?

EMILIA. Poison him!

GLADYS. If he would only get angry!

EMILIA. If he would only talk back!

GLADYS. But he won't. Oh, Emilia! Really I am be- ginning to feel desperate. Can you think of nothing?

EMILIA. Richard!

GLADYS. Richard!—Pshaw!

EMILIA. " Pshaw? "

GLADYS. Well—but of what use can Richard be?

EMILIA. Well, Gladys, I must declare——

GLADYS. But, if Mr. Wyncot has the law on his side, not all the Richards in the world can alter it; and what is impossible, is impossible.

EMILIA. Then, you think of submitting?

GLADYS. " Submitting? " (*emphasis of sarcastic sur- prise*)

EMILIA. No! You don't. Gladys, you are a girl of spirit. But you are peculiar. Yes, you are. And so am I—though in a different way. Now, you perhaps, would go out and drown yourself. But, that wouldn't spite him. What *we* want is to induce *him* to drown himself. And for that purpose——

(*The door, C., suddenly opens, and* RICHARD JOCELYN *appears on the threshold.*)

Richard! The very person!—Come in!

RICHARD. (*in repressed tones, tragically*) Breathe not my name! (*he turns and closes the door behind him, quickly and cautiously*)

EMILIA. (*amazed*) Why, what's the matter?

RICHARD. (*advancing*) Ah, well may you ask! (*to* GLADYS) Miss Wyncot, pardon this rude intrusion! Your Cerberus is on guard, but I appeased him with a bone.

EMILIA. (*amazed and alarmed*) Richard Jocelyn!—in the name of goodness——

RICHARD. Hear me, then! I would not reproach you, but, O, Emilia! I have observed your advice—and behold the results!

EMILIA. *My* advice?

RICHARD. I have been " respectful—but firm."

EMILIA. And you have had trouble with papa?

RICHARD. "Trouble?" Well, in his own classic phrase, "possibly!—per'aps! " Emilia, I have been notified to quit.

EMILIA. Discharged? O, Richard! (*she falls into his arms*)

RICHARD. (*upholding* EMILIA) Don't cry, Miss Wyncot!

GLADYS. Well, really, Mr. Jocelyn, I am very, very sorry.

RICHARD. I believe you, Miss Wyncot. Women like to be sorry.

(EMILIA *recovers, and disengages herself.*)

No offence! " But what are tears to a grief like mine? " Yes, Emilia, I am not " indispensable." Or, so it appears. At all events, your papa has dispensed with me —and seemingly without a pang! Only to think! But yesterday—— (*taking card from his pocket, displays it, and reads*) " Richard Jocelyn—with—Joseph Jekyll, Attorney." Seven and six, for that! Engraved plate, and a hundred Bristol boards! And now, farewell! " Farewell, fond dream! " (*tossing away the card*) Emilia, fare-thee-well!

EMILIA. And where are you going?

RICHARD. (*despairingly*) " Going? "

EMILIA. Yes—hadn't you thought of that? And what do you propose to do?

RICHARD. Emilia, there is a schooner in the cove, with full cargo—ready to sail—and I hear she is short of hands. "The world is wide," we are told, Emilia.

EMILIA. Absurd! You are out of your head.

RICHARD. Granted!

EMILIA. Now listen to me! As for papa, whatever he may say, and whatever he may *do*, he will come around. You will see. Take my word for it!

RICHARD. (*with apprehensive glance toward door, c.*) "Come around?"

EMILIA. Well, you know what I mean. And it shall be soon, too. That I promise you.

RICHARD. Ah, if I had but your courage, Emilia!

EMILIA. Gladys! may he trust me?

GLADYS. Well, I certainly think so.

EMILIA. *I* know papa. Just leave him to me! Don't go near him, for the present! Let him rest!

RICHARD. "Let him rest?" "Requiescat in pace!" If that is all you require, Emilia——

EMILIA. But, meantime, of course, you want some occupation—if only to divert your mind.

RICHARD. Well said!

EMILIA. And to help you to that, I have an idea——

RICHARD. Another? Emilia!

EMILIA. Now, don't be alarmed!—for this time, I am sure, it is a good one. Not precisely in the way of business—but it may lead to something.

RICHARD. Lead on!

EMILIA. Well, then—first, you must know that Mr. Wyncot has just been here, and has acted outrageously.

(BUTTONS *thrusts in his head, door c., unobserved, and becomes an interested listener.*)

RICHARD. "Outrageously?"

EMILIA. Indeed, has insulted us both.

GLADYS. Emilia!

EMILIA. Well, I'm sure, Gladys——

GLADYS. But you must tell it as it was.

EMILIA. Now don't attempt to soften it!

(GLADYS, *with warning gesture, checks* EMILIA, *calling attention to* BUTTONS.)

RICHARD. (*turning on* BUTTONS) Wretched boy! Avaunt!

(BUTTONS *vanishes.*—RICHARD *closes the door, quickly, and returns.*)

Now, ladies!—speak! (*grasping a wrist of each*) But, one at a time! You have been insulted. How? Propound!

EMILIA. Richard, it is impossible——

RICHARD. Impossible?

EMILIA. To reduce it to your comprehension——

RICHARD. Ah!

EMILIA. But, suffice it to say, he could not have acted worse.

RICHARD. "He could not have acted worse." You indorse that statement, Miss Wyncot?

GLADYS. Oh, Emilia!

RICHARD. Proceed!

EMILIA. Now, this is what I propose—you shall call him to account.

RICHARD. Account?

EMILIA. Yes.

RICHARD. Cold lead—and hot coffee—for two?

EMILIA. (*impatiently*) No!

RICHARD. Ah! I see. (*tucking up his cuffs*)

GLADYS. (*protestingly*) Mr. Jocelyn!

EMILIA. But, of course, you will go only far enough to frighten him, and give him to understand that we have a protector.

GLADYS. And suppose he should refuse to be frightened!

RICHARD. Yes! Suppose it, Emilia!

EMILIA. It is not supposable. Why, I could frighten him, myself.

RICHARD. I believe you, Emilia.

EMILIA. And besides, if he *should* give you trouble—which is simply a remote possibility——

RICHARD. Ah! Let us hope so.

EMILIA. But, if he should, and they were even to arrest you——

GLADYS. Emilia!

EMILIA. Well, at the worst, you can plead your own case—and so you will have a client.

RICHARD. Emilia, it *is* an idea.

GLADYS. Emilia, it is simply absurd. And Mr. Jocelyn, I forbid you to think of it for a moment.

RICHARD. Allow me! Miss Wyncot, I respect your scruples; but justice must be vindicated. The question is simply this:—You are absolutely sure that the provocation has been sufficient?

EMILIA. Yes!

RICHARD. Yes?

GLADYS. No! No!

RICHARD. No?

EMILIA. Richard, as I have already said——

RICHARD. "He could not have acted worse." Tell me no more! And he is here?

EMILIA. (*pointing* L.) Yes. H'sh!

RICHARD. Ladies, you will oblige me by vacating the room immediately.

GLADYS. Never! Never! Never!

EMILIA. Now, Gladys, don't be a goose.

RICHARD. No, don't, Miss Wyncot. Be a duck.

EMILIA. As though anything serious could come of it!

GLADYS. Serious?

EMILIA. Why, of course he will apologize.

GLADYS. He? Mr. Wyncot?

EMILIA. When he sees Richard?

RICHARD. Why, of course!

GLADYS. But, if I could only be sure of that!

RICHARD. Ah—if *I* could only be sure! But we waste time.

EMILIA. Listen! He is coming.

GLADYS. Emilia!——

RICHARD. Ladies!—— (*urging them to door,* C.)

GLADYS. But you will be very careful, Mr. Jocelyn? —If only for your own sake!

RICHARD. I promise you.

GLADYS. But, O, Emilia!——

RICHARD. Go!

(*Exeunt,* GLADYS *and* EMILIA, *door* C., *pushed out by* RICHARD.)

" Thus bad begins—but worse remains behind."

(*Enter* WYNCOT, *door* L.; *he is in riding costume, and walks slowly forward, absorbed in a document which he carries in his hand.* RICHARD *observes him, and comments, aside.*)

Sizeable sort of chap! Biceps apparently well developed! But out of training! Sir!

WYNCOT. (*glancing up*) Good-morning! Good-morning! (*eyes again on paper*)

RICHARD. Doesn't seem impressed. (*offering card*) Permit me——

WYNCOT. (*taking card*) Ah! Your card?

(RICHARD *bows,* WYNCOT *reads card.*)

" Richard Jocelyn."—Indeed? "With Joseph Jekyll "——

RICHARD. Permit me, again. (*retaking card, writes on it with pencil*)

WYNCOT. With pleasure! (*receives the card again from* RICHARD) Ah! I perceive. (*reads*) "*Without* Joseph Jekyll."

RICHARD. I have dispensed with him.

WYNCOT. You are then of the legal persuasion?

RICHARD. I am.

WYNCOT. And 'isengaged.

RICHARD. Very much so.

WYNCOT. Well, sir, I am glad to meet you. How can I serve you?

RICHARD. Ah! The question is a leading one.

WYNCOT. Pardon me!

RICHARD. But it possesses, at least, the virtue of directness. Sir, you can place me under lasting obligations, by making me the defendant in an action for assault and battery.

WYNCOT. I fail to comprehend.

RICHARD. I shall be glad to enlighten you. You have offended, sir, a certain young lady——

WYNCOT. Oh! There is a lady in the case?

RICHARD. Strictly speaking, two.

WYNCOT. That complicates matters.

RICHARD. Seriously.—I may add, sir, to be exact, that I have not the remotest conception of what you have done; but I am credibly informed that you "could not have acted worse."

WYNCOT. So? And you are here— -

RICHARD. As their representative——

WYNCOT. To receive an explanation.

RICHARD. The case is respectfully submitted.

WYNCOT. Well, sir, this is awkward.

RICHARD. I can believe it.

WYNCOT. Exceedingly so! You couldn't be prevailed upon to sit down?

RICHARD. No! Thank you!

WYNCOT. No—under the circumstances, it would not, perhaps, be proper. (*musingly.—Seats himself,* L. C., *and regards* RICHARD, *critically*) But, upon my word, Mr. Jocelyn, this *is* awkward—and unfortunate.

RICHARD. It is likely to prove so—to one of us.

WYNCOT. Possibly to both. For, by a most remarkable coincidence, I was just at this moment setting forth, in search of legal advice.

RICHARD. (*suddenly interested*) "Advice?" "Legal?"

WYNCOT. And I am particularly desirous of finding an adviser, who is *not* "with Joseph Jekyll, attorney."

RICHARD. Indeed, sir?—With your permission, I *will* sit down.

WYNCOT. I think there is nothing in "the code" that forbids it.

RICHARD. (*seating himself, tentatively, R. C.*) Thank you! "Legal advice!"

WYNCOT. Yes! You see, Mr. Jocelyn—if I may so trouble you——

RICHARD. (*hitching his chair a little closer*) Pray, proceed!

WYNCOT. I have certain accounts, which require immediate inspection. And I am also called upon to take action in certain matters involving legal questions, with which I am but imperfectly acquainted. Now, all this, I daresay, is precisely in your line?

RICHARD. "Line," sir! My "line?"

WYNCOT. You have received a legal education?

RICHARD. Of the best.

WYNCOT. Of which you could furnish certificates?

RICHARD. Unquestionable.

WYNCOT. And are, besides, acquainted with the books of this estate?

RICHARD. From A. to Z.

WYNCOT. How very unfortunate!

RICHARD. Excuse me?

WYNCOT. I said, "How very unfortunate!" For if, now, you were at liberty to accept——

RICHARD. (*recoiling*) Ah! True! (*aside*) Emilia!

WYNCOT. And then, too, I don't mind telling you, Mr. Jocelyn, that I am much pleased with your appearance.

RICHARD. Oh, thank you, sir!

WYNCOT. Though being a stranger in the neighborhood, I am, of course, liable to be deceived.

RICHARD. Oh, certainly!

WYNCOT. However, I should take the chances. And if upon trial, you were to prove to be what I think you—well—the question of salary should never separate us.

RICHARD. Oh!—my dear sir!

WYNCOT. If only you were at liberty to accept!

RICHARD. Of course! "If!" (*the "If," in an agonized aside*) Then, why mention it?

WYNCOT. True! All this is superfluous—I suppose.

RICHARD. But, excuse me, sir!—Does it not occur to you—since you seem to regret my disability—that—(*hesitating*)

WYNCOT. Well?

RICHARD. That you, sir, might easily remove it?

WYNCOT. I?

RICHARD. By a few, simple, inexpensive words. A mere—apology——

WYNCOT. " Apology? "

RICHARD. Or, something, of that innocuous sort.—I merely suggest it.

WYNCOT. (*musingly*) Ah, yes!—Yes, it has occurred to me.

RICHARD. (*aside*) It has occurred to him.

WYNCOT. And I am sorry—sincerely——

RICHARD. (*interrupting, and springing to his feet*) " Sorry? " I knew it, sir. Say no more! (*offering his hand*)

WYNCOT. But I fear you misapprehend me. I am sorry—that I cannot quite see my way to such an adjustment.

RICHARD. (*crushed, but with dignity*) Pray don't distress yourself! (*aside*) O, hapless Emilia!

(*Turning again on* WYNCOT, *with air of sad but stern resolve.*)

Then, sir, but one thing remains, it would seem——

WYNCOT. (*interrupting*) But, before we proceed to extremities—does it not occur to *you*, Mr. Jocelyn, that in undertaking the role of champion, without the " remotest conception " of the cause, you are acting somewhat impulsively? And, rather from gallantry and good-nature—possibly—than from good judgment?

RICHARD. Why—well—yes! Yes, sir—upon reflection—it does begin to occur.

WYNCOT. And might it not be wise, in the circumstances—I merely suggest it—to try negotiations, before resorting to hostilities?

RICHARD. Sir, the suggestion strikes me most favorably—I may say, forcibly.

WYNCOT. (*consulting watch*) I can spare a few minutes. How is it with you?

RICHARD. I have time to consume, sir.

WYNCOT. (*rising, and extending his hand*) Mr. Jocelyn, to the best of my belief, you are a good fellow—and we shall yet be good friends.

RICHARD. (*grasping his hand*) Sir, to the best of *my* belief, you are another; and I have a vacancy on the list of my friends.

EMILIA. (*without—door* c.—*heard faintly*) Oh!

(RICHARD *starts, and glances toward door,* c.)

WYNCOT. (*striking bell on table*) One moment!

(*Enter* BUTTONS, *door*, C.)

Buttons!

BUTTONS. Yessir——

WYNCOT. Where are the young ladies?

BUTTONS. Listenin' at the key-'ole, sir.

(*A slight feminine scream is heard from without door*, C.)

WYNCOT. Very good! Remember my instructions!

(*To* RICHARD, *throwing open door*, L. 1.)

Will you walk into the library? We shall be more private.

(RICHARD *hesitates for a moment, glancing toward door*, C.)

RICHARD. (*with determination*) I will, sir.

(*Exit* RICHARD, *door*, L. 1.)

WYNCOT. (*to* BUTTONS) Tell the ladies they may come in.

(*Exit* WYNCOT, *door*, L. 1., *following* RICHARD.)

. BUTTONS. (*facing up stage—shouts*) You may come hin.

(*Enter*, EMILIA *and* GLADYS, *door* C. *They pause just within doorway.*)

EMILIA. (*to* BUTTONS) Oh!—Oh, you young *monster!*

GLADYS. How dare you? You shameless, ungrateful boy!

EMILIA. (*advancing on* BUTTONS) Gladys, I could strangle him—I could.

(BUTTONS *sidles toward door*, R. 2.)

GLADYS. (*restraining* EMILIA) But, don't! For if you touch him, he will simply screech for his " mamma;" and then we shall have *her* about our ears.

BUTTONS. (*retreating, backward*) Yes'm.

EMILIA. " Yes'm," indeed! (*she darts at* BUTTONS)

BUTTONS. Mamma! (*he plunges out door*, R. 2.)

EMILIA. Gladys!—what *shall* be done?

GLADYS. Don't ask me! To have robbed us of our only friend!

EMILIA. But, at least we have each other. (*she falls into* GLADYS's *arms*)

GLADYS. (*embracing her*) And we will never separate?

EMILIA. Never!

GLADYS. Not even if Richard——

EMILIA. (*freeing herself*) Richard! Never let me hear his name again! Gladys, I have his picture at home—and do you know what I shall do with it? I shall give it to the cook.—Yes! and I shall have her paste it in the receipt-book, among the muffins—where it belongs.

(*Noise of slamming doors, without.*)

Gracious! What's that?

JEKYLL. (*without—shouting*) 'Ello! James! Mr. Wyncot! 'Ello!

EMILIA. Why, it is papa.

JEKYLL. (*without—nearer*) 'Ello, there! 'Ello!

(*Enter, rapidly,* JEKYLL, *followed by* Jon, *door*, C. JEKYLL *continues to shout.*)

Mr. Wyncot! W'ere is 'e? Hemilia!—don't answer, but speak!

GLADYS. (*alarmed*) Mr. Wyncot? In the library.

JEKYLL. (*circling about the room*) In the liberary?—And w'ere is the liberary?

GLADYS. (*springing toward door,* L. 1.) Here!

EMILIA. But, mercy upon us! Papa——

JEKYLL. (*pounding on door,* L. 1.) 'Ello! 'Ello!

EMILIA. Is the house on fire?

(*Enter* MRS. PRINGLE, *leading* BUTTONS, *door* R. 2. *She pauses in astonishment.*)

JEKYLL. (*pounding on door, and shouting, with increased vigor*) 'Ello!—I say.

(*The door,* L. 1, *opens, and* WYNCOT *appears.* JEKYLL *falls back, removing his hat.*)

Ho! Bless my 'eart! Well!—'ere you are, sir!

WYNCOT. Mr. Jekyll! What now? You seem excited.

JEKYLL. "Hexcited?" 'Old this, Mr. Job!

(*Gives his hat to* JON—*panting, and mopping his face with bandanna.*)

Well, sir! Now, sir! 'Ark'ee, sir!—and let us 'ear wot you'll say to this! Sir, we 'ave delivered your overtures to the men——

WYNCOT. Ah! You have.

JEKYLL. We 'ave, sir, *verbatim*;—and they reject them, sir, *hin toto*.

WYNCOT. Is it possible?

JEKYLL. *Hin toto!*

JOB. (*anxious to contribute to the information*) Ay, sir! And wot is more, sir——

JEKYLL. (*brushing* JOB *aside*) Hexcuse me! And wot is more, sir, they 'ave looted the *magazine*.

JOB. Dear! dear!

WYNCOT. The magazine!

JEKYLL. The hentire outfit—powder, *and* dynamite!

JOB. Ay, sir!—not forgettin' the dynamite!

JEKYLL. And at noon, sir, *precisely*, of this very day—unless in the meantime they 'ear from you further——

WYNCOT. Well?

JEKYLL. Well, sir—*hup* goes the power-'ouse!

WYNCOT. The power-house?

JOB. 'Tis Gospel truth, sir!

JEKYLL. Hup it goes. And wot'll go next, if you 'old to your present course, 'Eaven knows!—but don't ask *me*, sir! Eh?—Mr. Job?

JOB. Ay!—truly, sir! Terrible it is, w'en the 'eathen rage!

WYNCOT. Well!—it would seem so—really! And how vigorously they go about it—in this case! Not to say, prematurely!

JEKYLL. (*smiling and bowing, in the character of vindicated oracle*) You'll remember, sir—per'aps——

WYNCOT. You told me so! True! Very true! (*consulting watch*) And I am allowed——

JEKYLL. (*pulling out watch*) Five minutes, sir—scant!

WYNCOT. Pardon me! You said, till noon.

JEKYLL. (*displaying his watch to* WYNCOT) Very well, sir! Five minutes!

WYNCOT. (*displaying his watch to* JEKYLL) Ten!—Not wishing to disparage your watch. But I think you are fast. We have full ten minutes.

JEKYLL. (*throwing up his hands*) And is this a time——

(*Turns to* JOB, *who shakes his head, dolefully.* *Turns again to* WYNCOT.)

Sir, I 'ave borne with this indifference, and 'ave endeavored to excuse it; but patience 'as its limits. Slight now my hadmonition—*persist* in your 'eadstrong career, and I wash my 'ands of the 'ole affair—presently, at once, and forever!

WYNCOT. So! This is your ultimatum, Mr. Jekyll! And you would desert me, in my extremity?

JEKYLL. " Desert," sir? But who can assist a man who will not assist 'imself?

WYNCOT. True, again! Quite so, Mr. Jekyll! And as I had anticipated something of the sort, I have endeavored to provide against it. (*throws open door,* L. 1) Mr. Jocelyn!—will you step this way?

JEKYLL. (*astounded*) Jocelyn? Jocelyn?

(*Enter* RICHARD, *door,* L. 1.)

WYNCOT. Mr. Jocelyn, this is Mr. Jekyll.

(RICHARD *bows stiffly.*)

JEKYLL. (*to* RICHARD) Wot, sir? You 'ere?
WYNCOT. Ah! You have met.
RICHARD. Professionally.
WYNCOT. Mr. Jocelyn, we have arrived at a crisis. Mr. Jekyll is displeased with my methods—unalterably so, I understand—— (*turning to* JEKYLL)
JEKYLL. Ha, sir! Well, sir——
WYNCOT. Just so! He therefore insists on resigning his position as my agent, and legal adviser. Will you, Mr. Jocelyn, accept that position?
RICHARD. Mr. Wyncot, with thanks!
WYNCOT. It is yours.
JEKYLL. Ho, sir! But, excuse me, sir——
WYNCOT. (*interrupting*) One moment! I beg——
JEKYLL. (*interrupting*) But, sir—my clerk, sir——
WYNCOT. Your clerk, Mr. Jekyll?
JEKYLL. W'y, sir, I discharged 'im, only this morning.
WYNCOT. Then, how can he be your clerk, sir?
JEKYLL. Eh? Ho! Bless my 'eart! (*mopping his face*)
WYNCOT. Allow me! Still further:—the books of the estate have been for a long time unbalanced. Now, Mr. Jekyll naturally desires that they should be inspected, immediately. Will you, Mr. Jocelyn, inspect them?

(RICHARD *bows assent.*)

JEKYLL. (*quickly*) Eh? Wot? No, sir! No, sir! Hi protest, sir.

WYNCOT. *You* protest?

JEKYLL. For I 'ave *not* resigned.

WYNCOT. What?

JEKYLL. No, sir! No, sir!

WYNCOT. (*protestingly*) Mr. Jekyll——

JEKYLL. Hi appeal to Mr. Job, sir.

WYNCOT. But you *propose* to?

JEKYLL. No, sir! Never!

WYNCOT. "Never?" Really, Mr. Jekyll——

JEKYLL. Sir, I am incapable of such a hact.

(WYNCOT *turns away.* JEKYLL. *follows closely, speaking rapidly.*)

"*Hif*," sir—"*hif*," I merely remarked—supposin' a case. "Hif" you *were* to persist, in a certain course—But w'y allude to it? For you will not. No! I feel it in my 'eart—late though the hour may be—you will 'eed my warnings.

WYNCOT. (*endeavoring to interrupt*) Pardon me——

JEKYLL. (*over-riding the interruption*) Once more——

(WYNCOT *again turns away—hopelessly.* JEKYLL, *striking an attitude, continues, with increased volubility, and rising emphasis.*)

Once more, I say, if only for the sake of 'im who *laid* this 'eavy charge upon me—your noble huncle, sir!—and in the name of that lamented man!—sir, I *hadjure* you——

(*A loud explosion, without, interrupts* JEKYLL'S *speech. The glass in the great window,* R. U. E., *is shattered, and fragments fall to the floor.* GLADYS *and* EMILIA *scream, simultaneously, and rush into each other's arms.* MRS. PRINGLE *and* BUTTONS *wildly clutch each other.* JEKYLL *recoils, colliding with* JOB, *who has crouched behind him; but immediately recovering himself, alarmed, yet elated, he cries:—*)

Eh? 'Ark to that! And look! (*pointing to the shattered window*)

WYNCOT. (*taking out watch*) Upon my life, you were right.

JEKYLL. (*with anticipative triumph*) Ha! Well, sir?
WYNCOT. (*gazing on the watch in his hand*) If that
means noon, I am five minutes slow.

(JEKYLL *collapses. He is caught and supported by* JOB.
WYNCOT *turns to* RICHARD.)

Mr. Jocelyn!—the campaign is begun.

(RICHARD *bows.*)

Picture.

CURTAIN.

———————

ACT III.

SCENE.—*A glen, sloping steeply from back to front, and
overshadowed by trees, which spring from ledges of
out-cropping rock, on either hand. A brook, entering
up* L., *descends by a series of cascades, over rocks, and
through ferns, and passes off,* R. 2. *A path skirts the
left bank of brook, from up* L., *where it enters, to* R. C.,
on a line with 2. *Here it crosses the brook, by means
of a rustic bridge, with hand-rail, and following the
right bank, disappears, with brook, at* R. 2. *A second
path, entering up* R., *connects with the first at* R. *end
of bridge. At* L. *front, in the face of a precipitous
cliff, the mouth of an abandoned mine, half concealed
by foliage. A low bank, in front of the mouth of mine,
and leading up to it, is overgrown with grass, inter-
spersed with weeds and wild flowers; and the whole
foreground is similarly carpeted. At* R. *front, the
trunk of a fallen tree, moss-encrusted; and immediately behind this, a clump of shrubbery. The path
that enters up* L. *descends, for the first few feet, with
a very steep incline.*

(GLADYS *and* EMILIA *discovered, at curtain, on ledge at
the foot of the first incline of the path, up* L. GLADYS
*is in advance. Both stand in attitudes of suspense,
listening.*)

GLADYS. Listen! Wasn't that a step?
EMILIA. No!
GLADYS. You are sure?

EMILIA. (*after a moment's pause—still listening*) He has lost us.—Or, *we* have lost *him*. The little wretch! And he will never dare to follow us here.

GLADYS. Why—what is there to be afraid of?

EMILIA. (*pointing back up path*) The hill. Do you suppose he will risk his precious fat carcass——

GLADYS. (*interrupting*) Come on!

(*She advances down path, with decision—*EMILIA *following. A confused sound, as of many voices, is heard, from without, off* R.—*distant and faint.* GLADYS *halts, and lifts her hand warningly.*)

But, listen!

EMILIA. (*impatient and distressed*) To what?— Gladys!——

(*The sound is repeated—scarcely audible.*)

GLADYS. Well—don't you hear?

EMILIA. (*listening*) The men—at the ruins.

GLADYS. "Ruins?"

EMILIA. Of the power-house.

GLADYS. (*startled*) Are we so near?

EMILIA. Just across the hill. You should know.

GLADYS. But, I hadn't thought. They seem rather noisy.

EMILIA. Enjoying themselves, I daresay. *I* don't blame them. Do you?

GLADYS. (*with decision*) No! Come on! (*again advancing down path*)

EMILIA. (*following*) But, I really believe you are frightened. And you will have *me* frightened, next.

GLADYS. "Next," indeed! (*arriving at bridge and halting*) But, which way, now?

EMILIA. Well—we are in the "Glen."

GLADYS. And shall we go on—to the "Cove?"

EMILIA. But why should we? He hasn't forbidden our going to the "Cove."

GLADYS. True! This is the spot. (*turning toward* L. *front*) And here is the cavern we were going to explore.

EMILIA. Ugh! Don't go near it. It looks snakey. (*crossing to log,* R. *front*) See! Here is our old seat.

GLADYS. (*inspecting the log, with misgivings*) But which is worse—snakes, or—bugs?

EMILIA. (*whipping the log with her handkerchief*) Pshaw! A few ants, and such things, won't hurt you.

4

GLADYS. (*gathering her skirts about her, and sitting on log*) Well?

EMILIA. (*sitting beside* GLADYS) There!—And now, Mr. Wyncot, what will you say to this?

GLADYS. But, it *isn't* so very nice. And perhaps he will never know that we have disobeyed him.

EMILIA. Don't worry!

GLADYS. You think he will?

EMILIA. If I have to tell him, myself.

GLADYS. Emilia!

EMILIA. Well, we shall see if he can run everything—and everybody. But, I suppose you have heard?——

GLADYS. What?

EMILIA. The latest?

GLADYS. No!

EMILIA. Didn't I tell you? He is looking for more trouble, it seems.

GLADYS. Really?

EMILIA. The men at the wharf won't handle the coal —what little there is to handle—and the skippers are afraid to touch it. So Mr. Wyncot has chartered a schooner—or brig, or something—and proposes to load it himself.

GLADYS. And sail it, too?

EMILIA. He is equal to it—or thinks so.

GLADYS. Poor fellow!

EMILIA. Why, Gladys!

GLADYS. Well, isn't *any* one to be pitied, who has such *enormous* self-conceit?

(*A medley of sounds, suggestive of a landslide, low at first, but rapidly increasing, is heard from without, off* L. U. E. *The girls start, and glance back, in alarm. Enter on path, up* L., BUTTONS, *stumbling and slipping, and accompanied by a small avalanche of displaced stones and pebbles. He clutches the overhanging branch of a tree. It supports him for an instant, then breaks; and he alights, in a sitting posture, on the ledge at the foot of the declivity.*)

BUTTONS. Umph! (*a grunt of mingled surprise and pain*).

EMILIA. (*with a gasp—in tones wrathful, but repressed*) Heavens! That imp of Satan!

(GLADYS *starts to rise, but* EMILIA *checks her.*)

Keep still! He hasn't seen us.

(BUTTONS *rises slowly, rubs the part affected, and turn-ing, gazes back at the scene of his mishap. Then, slowly facing to the front, he peers about the glen. The shrubbery, at back of the log, for a brief time, serves to conceal the girls from his view. Suddenly he espies them. Thrusting his hands in his pockets, he gives vent to a low whistle of satisfaction, and a complacent smile spreads over his countenance. The girls rise.* EMILIA *speaks:*—)

Gladys, this is too much.

GLADYS. (*moving rapidly toward* L. *front*) Come on!

EMILIA. But, where are you going?—Not into that hole in the ground?

GLADYS. It's the only place where he won't follow.

EMILIA. But he will wait outside—till the day of Judgment.

GLADYS. (*halting*) That's true—I daresay.

EMILIA. We may as well have it out here. Sit down! (*in lower tones*) I have an idea.

(GLADYS *looks at her, distrustfully.*)

Now, don't quote Richard to me. But sit down!—and pay no attention to him.

(GLADYS *reluctantly seats herself on bank,* L. *front.* EMILIA *sits beside her, and continues in undertone.*)

We shall get rid of him. Only help me a little.

(BUTTONS, *still keeping his eyes fixed on the girls, moves cautiously down to bridge.*)

GLADYS. (*glancing toward* BUTTONS) Here he comes.

EMILIA. Look pleasant. (*turns her head, and ad-dresses* BUTTONS) Oh! is that you, Buttons? Glad to see you. Make yourself comfortable!

GLADYS. Well, if you fancy that sarcasm will affect him——

EMILIA. (*in undertone*) Keep quiet! (*in louder tones, for* BUTTONS' *ear*) Gladys, did you bring your em-broidery? (*taking needle-work from her pocket, as she speaks*)

GLADYS. No!

EMILIA. Then, you can help me with mine. (*plying her needle, and continuing to speak for* BUTTONS' *bene-fit*) Awfully kind of Mr. Wyncot, to send Buttons to protect us! Wasn't it? And awfully good of Buttons to come—at the risk of his neck—and other portions of his anatomy!

(BUTTONS, *still watchful of the girls, seats himself on hand-rail of bridge, his feet dangling over the water*.)

GLADYS. (*in undertone, after glancing toward* BUTTONS) He is taking your advice—making himself comfortable.

EMILIA. (*in undertone, continuing to stitch*) Never mind! (*again raising her voice*) But one thing, Gladys, we quite forgot—*luncheon!* And how stupid! For it was all but time for it, when we came away; and Heaven knows when we shall get back. Really, I am afraid we shall all be famished. Especially, poor Buttons! And I should be sorry to be the cause of his death —from starvation.

GLADYS. (*in protest—half amused, but hopeless*) Oh!

EMILIA. (*lifting a warning finger*) Sh!

(BUTTONS, *suddenly grown ruminative, heaves a profound sigh*. EMILIA *speaks, in undertone, but triumphantly*.)

Well? You hear?

GLADYS. (*in undertone—surprised*) Really?

EMILIA. (*in undertone*) "What a sigh was that!" It takes.

GLADYS. (*in undertone, incredulously—stealing a glance at* BUTTONS) *Cån that boy be hungry?*

EMILIA. (*in undertone*) Always! What did I tell you? Be careful!

(BUTTONS *passes his hands over the front of his jacket, which is abnormally distended*.)

GLADYS. (*in undertone, observant of* BUTTONS) He does seem distressed—but it can't be from emptiness.

EMILIA. (*confidently, in undertone*) You will see. He is as good as gone. (*stitching diligently, and again raising her voice*) Upon my word, Gladys, why *didn't* we think to bring at least a sandwich? Or, a big red apple or two, from Buttons' favorite tree? Or, better yet, one of those delicious ham-pies that your cook makes a specialty of, and Buttons appreciates above everything! I noticed one on the side-board, just as we came away—hot from the oven! And, oh, my!—to think that we shall not taste it!

(*While* EMILIA *is speaking,* BUTTONS *draws a pasty from under his jacket, and eyes it affectionately.*)

GLADYS. (*noting* BUTTONS' *performance, with half-real, half-assumed dismay, and laying her hand on* EMILIA'S *arm, as the latter finishes her speech*) No! I am really afraid we sha'n't.

EMILIA. (*looking up at* GLADYS, *bewildered*) Why—— What——

GLADYS. Look!

(EMILIA *looks, gasps, and is speechless.*)

The pie!

(BUTTONS, *from a pocket of his trousers, produces c sandwich.*)

And the sandwich!

(BUTTONS, *from another pocket, extracts an apple, large, and red; and immediately matches it with another.*)

And the "big, red apple!—or two! " Emilia, you were simply calling off his *menu.*

EMILIA. (*starting to rise*) This, certainly, is the limit.

GLADYS. (*pulling her back*) Oh, no, it isn't. See!

(BUTTONS, *from various hiding-places in his clothing, brings forth additional eatables, which he piles on his lap.*)

More, yet!

EMILIA. In the name of goodness, where does it all come from?

GLADYS. And where is it all going to?

(BUTTONS *begins his feast, biting into the pasty.*)

EMILIA. Gladys, do you think he could be coaxed?

GLADYS. You might try, Emilia.

EMILIA. (*rising and calling*) Buttons!—Buttons!— Are you so very angry with me?

BUTTONS. (*busily eating*) Yes'm!

EMILIA. But you know if I did call you names, it was only in fun—don't you?

BUTTONS. (*mouth full—interrogatively*) Uh? (*then, affirmatively, but indifferently*) Uh-huh!

EMILIA. And besides, if you *don't* like *me*, you are fond of your mistress—who has been so good to you—aren't you? And you would be glad to do something to please her, I'm sure.

BUTTONS (*between bites*) Yes'm!

EMILIA. Gladys, he is not so bad, after all. (*again to* BUTTONS) Then, if she were to ask you to go away and leave us, you would go, wouldn't you?

BUTTONS. (*in the same tone as before*) No'm!

GLADYS. (*hopelessly*) Emilia, it is not worth while.

EMILIA. There is just one chance left. (*takes coin from her pocket*) Buttons! Do you see this? And do you know what it is? (*holding up coin, and advancing toward him*)

(BUTTONS' *jaws cease to wag, and he eyes the coin, with interest.*)

Oh, have a good look! (*she moves nearer, and holds the coin before his eyes*)

BUTTONS. It's a Brummagem.

EMILIA. No, it isn't, you suspicious little wretch! It's a good, whole half-crown.

GLADYS. Emilia! He isn't worth it.

EMILIA. (*continuing, to* BUTTONS) And it's all yours, if you will go straight away, this minute, and not come back. Do you hear?

BUTTONS. (*extending his hand for the coin*) Yes'm.

EMILIA. But you will go? You promise—solemnly—and 'pon honor?

BUTTONS. Yes'm.

EMILIA. Remember, now!—There! (*she drops coin in* BUTTONS' *hand, and turns to* GLADYS) And cheap enough!

BUTTONS. (*trys coin between his teeth, and pockets it*) Thank'ee, m'm! (*he calmly resumes his feast*)

EMILIA. Well! Put away your provisions—and vacate! Make haste!

GLADYS. He's putting them away.

EMILIA. (*excitedly*) But aren't you going?

BUTTONS. (*placidly, sampling an apple*) No'm.

GLADYS. (*rising*) Oh, Emilia!

EMILIA. (*with growing excitement and wrath*) You're not? And didn't you just promise that you would —solemnly—and 'pon honor?

BUTTONS. Yes'm.

EMILIA. Gladys!—don't say a word! (*again to* BUTTONS) Then, when you made that promise, you simply told a horrid, wilful, wicked, deliberate lie—did you?

BUTTONS. (*unmoved*) Yes'm.

EMILIA. (*rushing upon him, in sudden fury, seizing him by the shoulders, and shaking him violently*) Oh! you young *Ananias!* There!

(*She finishes with a push which dislodges him from the rail.* BUTTONS *falls into the water—disappearing, with splash, behind bank.*)

GLADYS. (*with shrick*) Oh! Emilia! you have drowned him.

EMILIA. (*rejoining* GLADYS) Gladys, I don't care.

(BUTTONS *is heard, splashing and spluttering in the water.*)

GLADYS. But listen! Horrors! (*she starts toward the pool.*)

EMILIA. (*restraining her*) Don't go near him! It isn't knee-deep.

BUTTONS. (*invisible—calling, frantically*) Mamma!

EMILIA. He lives.

BUTTONS. (*climbing into view*) Mamma! Mamma!

(*Gaining the bank, he casts one reproachful look on the girls; then, turning, rushes up the path, arms extended, clambers up the final steep, and disappears,* L. U. E.—*calling as he goes:*—)

Mamma! Mamma!

(*His voice dies away in the distance.*)

EMILIA. Well—you see, Gladys! *Some* things can be done—as well as others!

GLADYS. (*agitated*) Yes!—But, Heavens!——

EMILIA. What's the matter?

GLADYS. Such a tragedy!—Almost!

EMILIA. But not quite—more's the pity! So no one need go into mourning.

GLADYS. No! On the contrary! I know of some one who will find it highly entertaining.

EMILIA. Meaning Mr. Wyncot, I suppose.

GLADYS. Or any one who hears of it. And, of course, *everybody will* hear.

BUTTONS. (*without — in remote distance — calling*) Mamma!

GLADYS. (*holding up her hand*) Listen! There he goes—yelling at every jump!

EMILIA. (*defiantly*) Well!—what of it? Who cares?

GLADYS. (*pacing, nervously*) Oh, not I—I am sure!

EMILIA. The odious little liar! What were boys made for, anyhow? See how he has splashed my gown!

GLADYS. (*suddenly pausing, lifting her hand, and listening*) Listen!

EMILIA. (*also listening*) To what?—Now, don't keep that up!

GLADYS. (*breaking her pose*) But *he* is keeping it up. They'll know all about it in the next county, before dinner.

EMILIA. (*exasperated*) Well, I hope to goodness they will! And if you are so afraid that "His Mightiness" won't approve of it, just refer him to me!

GLADYS. "Afraid?" I? That *who* won't approve? "His Mightiness," indeed!

EMILIA. Oh, very well, Gladys! But you've done nothing but distress yourself about him—and sympathize with him—and *apologize* for him—ever since we came out.

GLADYS. Well, upon my word!

EMILIA. And I should think, after driving poor Richard away, you might at least have the grace——

GLADYS. (*interrupting*) Emilia! Is there anything *else* you can accuse me of? But the idea! That you should hold *me* to blame for Richard's shameful desertion of you!

EMILIA. "Desertion!" Thank you! But it was on your account that it happened—you'll admit.

GLADYS. Really! And you are sorry. I see. And *I* am sorry. And I will humbly entreat Richard——

EMILIA. (*hotly interrupting*) Indeed, you will do nothing of the sort! I'll have you to understand, Gladys, that I am quite capable of attending to my own affairs; and, as for Richard, if he prefers Mr. Wyncot's company to ours, he may have my blessing to go with it!

GLADYS. Oh, I hear you blessing him, now.

EMILIA. But I did expect you to show some little appreciation——

GLADYS. (*interrupting*) Of the sacrifice! And so I should have done. Emilia. But how was I to know that you were mourning for him? Only this morning, you called him—What was it?—A "muffin," if my memory serves me.

EMILIA. (*catching her breath*) Did I? What a memory you must have!

GLADYS. Now, Emilia, you are losing your temper—and you know it doesn't become you.

EMILIA. Well, Gladys, I must say, when you *wish* to be agreeable, you can certainly be the *most* agreeable——

GLADYS. (*interrupting, and turning away*) Come! Let us go back! We have simply made ourselves ridiculous.

EMILIA. And it's all my fault?

GLADYS. Have I said so?

EMILIA. You might as well.

GLADYS. (*glancing up the pati*) I suppose we're not likely to meet any one. Still, if you care to know, your hat is on crooked, and your hair is coming down.

EMILIA. (*explosively*) Oh!

(*Further words failing her, she sets her hat right, with a jerk, turns, and marches rapidly up path.*)

GLADYS. (*calling after her*) Emilia!—Emilia! you have forgotten your work. (*picking up needle-work, which* EMILIA *has dropped*)

(EMILIA, *unheeding, mounts the path, and vanishes,* L. U. E.)

She has really gone!—What a happy ending—to our beautifully-planned excursion! And how *he* will enjoy it!—and comment on it! But not to me!—for I will never go back! Never! At least, not till—— (*pausing, and casting a doubtful glance about her*) What a horrid place! And how we could ever have fancied that we liked it—Really, this is the meanest act that Emilia was ever guilty of!—to leave me, in such a bear's den! And to go—up that frightful path—is just about as bad as to stay.

(*The snapping of a branch is heard, from without, off* L. U. E. GLADYS *starts, and listens. A displaced stone rolls down the first declivity of path.*)
Ah! She is coming back. She has thought better of it. Oh, very good, miss! But you sha'n't find *me* anxious—or on the look-out.

(*She goes quickly to log,* R., *seats herself, and begins stitching on* EMILIA'S *embroidery.*)

And perhaps you fancy that I will be the first to speak——

(*Enter, on path, up* L., WYNCOT, *in pedestrian costume; lighted cigarette, in mouth; slender cane in hand. He steps lightly and quickly from entrance, down the first declivity, and pauses on ledge.* GLADYS, *hearing the sound of his approach, tosses her head, shrugs her shoulders—but keeps her face carefully averted—and remarks, in low tones, to herself:—*)

We shall see!

(*She busies herself with the embroidery.* WYNCOT, *standing on the ledge, takes the cigarette from his mouth, blows out a puff of smoke, and remains motionless, regarding her. Bending over the embroidery, she sings, to herself, in low tones, carelessly, and brokenly—the measure at times delayed by the difficulty which she experiences with the stitches:—*)

" Oh, where are you going, my pretty maid? "
" I'm going a-milking—sir,"—she said.

(*Tugging at thread, breaks off, with impatient exclamation.*)

Ugh! What a snarl!

(WYNCOT, *smiling, slowly descends path, toward her.*)

And I never could untangle—anything!

(*She snaps the thread, and begins industriously rethreading her needle—singing, the while, brokenly, as before:—*)

"May I go with you—my pretty—maid? "
" You're kindly welcome—sir "——

(*Breaking off, and biting the end of her thread.*)

WYNCOT. (*who has arrived near her—supplying the lacking words*) " She said."
GLADYS. (*springing to her feet, in confusion*) Oh!
WYNCOT. And how good of her! Well—shall we be going?

(*Bowing, and offering his arm.* GLADYS *surveys him, with a sweeping, indignant glance, and turns away.*)

Sorry to interrupt so charming a performance; but you are ready, I trust, to follow your friend?

(*With a decided movement, she re-seats herself on the log.*)

Ah! Not all "pretty maids" are as gracious as she of the ditty.

GLADYS. (*haughtily, with glance toward him*) I had supposed, sir——

WYNCOT. That you were quite deserted? And *I* had supposed—from the appearance of Miss Jekyll, as she passed me on the path——

(GLADYS *tosses her head, and again busies herself with needle-work.*)

Yes, it was really quite alarming. I almost feared that I might find you in distress. But I was mistaken, it seems. Very much so!—Quite sufficient to yourself? *Fond* of solitude—and self-communion?

GLADYS. (*snappishly*) Very!

WYNCOT. (*looking about him*) Well, the spot seems well chosen for the purpose. Also, in other respects, quite worthy of its reputation. Creeping things rather numerous, I suspect. However—Pardon me!

(*Interrupting himself, bending above her, and picking an object from the brim of her hat. She shrinks back, glancing up at him.*)

Don't be alarmed! Merely a caterpillar!

GLADYS. (*with start, and shiver*) Ugh!

WYNCOT. But, on the whole, a very pleasant spot. Picturesque, decidedly! Rocks! and trees! and—What have we here?

(*Observing the mouth of mine, L. front, and crossing toward it.*)

The mouth of an old working—I should say—abandoned. Even here commercialism has not scrupled to intrude, and mar the face of Nature. But, the venture didn't pay, apparently. Fortunately, for you!

GLADYS. (*meaningly, with side-glance*) There are other ventures, sir, that are not paying.

WYNCOT. True! *Unfortunately!* Or, perhaps you regard that, too, as fortunate?

GLADYS. The loss is yours, sir.

WYNCOT. And that you find a consolation. Well, I am not, it would seem, at present, adding greatly to my store—either of fortune or friends. But, have you anything to suggest? Any means, or method, by which the condition might be improved?

GLADYS. You would listen?—of course!

WYNCOT. I have always been accounted a good listener.

GLADYS. (*with intense sarcasm*) No doubt! To listen requires no great effort.

WYNCOT. Come! Isn't that rather cruel? You have an opinion, evidently; and I should be very pleased to hear it. (*again approaching her, persuasively*) But we might talk about that as we walk along.

GLADYS. You will excuse me for declining to discuss the subject.

WYNCOT. Ah!

GLADYS. (*busy with embroidery*) Also, for declining to walk.

WYNCOT. (*with glance backward, and around him*) Well!—you can hardly expect to be carried.

GLADYS. (*intensely indignant—half rising*) Sir!

WYNCOT. Yet, in one way, or another, I think it highly advisable——

GLADYS. (*interrupting*) You have once before, sir, condescended to inform me as to what you think "advisable," in the matter of my going and coming——

WYNCOT. (*interrupting*) True! And very ill-advised it was, on my part.

GLADYS. I think so.

WYNCOT. For it accounts, probably, for your being here. But you were about to say——

GLADYS. (*piqued*) I was about to say, sir, that as an Englishwoman, I object to having my liberties restricted, without good and sufficient cause; and am accustomed to having such *advice* accompanied with reasons. You may have found the ladies of India more amenable to discipline.

WYNCOT. I was never legally responsible for any of the ladies of India.

GLADYS. (*with toss of head*) Ah, indeed! "Legally!"

WYNCOT. But you really insist upon a reason, in this case?

(GLADYS *shrugs her shoulders, and continues to stitch.*)

Not, of course, for information; but simply as a matter of prerogative.

GLADYS. I may tell you, sir, that above all things I detest sarcasm.

WYNCOT. Most women do. However, I will gladly oblige. To be explicit, then:—the neighborhood is not as peaceful as it might be; the men are idle, and not in the most lamb-like of humors; and some of them, I regret to say, have been drinking rather heavily, during the day.

GLADYS. All of which might have been avoided.

WYNCOT. Possibly! But that is a digression. The logic of the case——

GLADYS. (*interrupting—snappishly*) And I detest *logic.*

WYNCOT. Most women do. You see, you are not peculiar—in all things.

GLADYS. (*with increased pique*) How thoroughly you are qualified to judge—no doubt!

WYNCOT. Well—I may have fancied so—once. But, candidly, I begin to doubt it. You have given me much food for thought, Miss Wyncot.—Serious, and perplexing thought.

GLADYS. Really! It is a pity, sir, that you can't find some more pleasant—and profitable—subject for study.

WYNCOT. I have not said that I find it unpleasant. Besides, I have certain obligations—as you know—of a very weighty nature.

GLADYS. (*rising quickly—with intense feeling*) As I *do* know, sir, only too well!—to my deep regret, as you have been told!—and to my very great distress, as you should see! Do you fancy that I am likely to forget it? —or that the "obligations" of which you complain, weigh less heavily on me, than on you?

WYNCOT. I have not meant to complain.

GLADYS. Oh, sir, be honest! We are both victims of an unfortunate arrangement, well intended, no doubt, but acceptable to neither of us—and to one of us, at least, as I may frankly tell you, *unbearable!*

WYNCOT. I am sorry.

GLADYS. But it is not enough to be sorry. Some way of escape must be found—for both of us—*immediately!* For, surely a way *can* be found?

WYNCOT. Well—let us hope so! If not "immediately," within a reasonable time.

GLADYS. Then use your superior intellect to some practical purpose, and find it! And, rest assured, sir, you shall have my assistance, in any and every possible way in which I can render it.

WYNCOT. You are very kind. But, meanwhile, I must

do what I can to meet my responsibilities. (*casting a look about and behind him*) And, once more——

(*Approaching her, as he speaks, and again deferentially offering his arm.* GLADYS *whirls quickly, re-seats herself stiffly on log, and looks away.* WYNCOT *also turns away, disappointedly, and self-reproachfully.*)

Ah. Why did I speak?

GLADYS. (*angrily, turning on him*) And do you propose, sir, to remain here, till I am ready to accompany you?

WYNCOT. " Man proposes," it has been said, Miss Wyncot—but woman——

GLADYS. (*interrupting, impatiently*) Yes! I have heard.

WYNCOT. *Opposes*—in most cases—doesn't she? Or, at all events, *disposes*. So says the adage; and, though somewhat irreverent, wouldn't it seem to be true?

GLADYS. An average specimen of man's wit! Not only irreverent, but silly!

WYNCOT. Indeed?

GLADYS. For, if it were true in this case——

(*She breaks off, with significant look at him.*)

WYNCOT. Ah! What would you do, Miss Wyncot? Candidly, now, if it were true—as indeed you may assume it is—what disposition would you make of this problem?—and incidentally of me?

GLADYS. And *you* can be in doubt?—with *your* expertness in reading the minds of my shallow-minded sex!

WYNCOT. Why will you accuse me of pretentions which I have just disclaimed?—and of which you have cured me? No! In all sincerity, Miss Wyncot, I would give much, at this moment, only to know, with reasonable certainty, what course I should take to please you.

GLADYS. (*giving him a glance, half-surprised, half-reproachful*) To " please " me! It doesn't occur to you that it would cost you nothing—but a little common courtesy—simply to take me at my word, and leave me?

WYNCOT. It does. But, even if my conscience would permit it, could I rely on your appreciating that courtesy? In fact, Miss Wyncot, I have but one clew, to assist me in guessing at your meanings and intentions: —that afforded by history.

GLADYS. (*with smiling sarcasm*) Indeed? I am a historical personage.

WYNCOT. No allusion to your age intended.

GLADYS. Oh! Thank you, sir!

WYNCOT. But historical you are. I may not understand the type—but I recognize it. And I am further reminded from my reading, that it has always caused trouble.

GLADYS. (*with surprised stare—drawing herself up*) Really, sir!

WYNCOT. Not wilfully, perhaps—in all cases; but invariably, from the days of Helen, down.

GLADYS. How flattering! To be compared with Helen!

WYNCOT. I feared you might regard it so. Most women do.

GLADYS. (*angered, but haughtily—springing to her feet*) And what role in history do you assign to yourself, sir?

WYNCOT. None! None, whatever!

GLADYS. Oh, sir! you are too modest. Or, perhaps you count on *making* history—with some *new* Helen?

WYNCOT. No!—unfortunately! If I were younger—more susceptible, and eligible—then perhaps——

GLADYS. (*dropping a mocking courtesy*) My compliments, sir! and apologies! Really, you have more discernment than I had credited you with. I think you may regard yourself as safe, sir.

WYNCOT. I fear so.

(GLADYS, *finishing her speech, sweeps toward c., as if to depart.* WYNCOT *interposes, preventing her passing.*)

But you are not going?

GLADYS. (*throwing back her head, and regarding him*) Since *you* will not! And since *I* cannot stop forever. But I require no escort; and this, at least, should be plain:—So long as we *must* endure the affliction of a relationship so odious to us both, we can henceforth best please and serve each other, simply by avoiding and ignoring each other.

WYNCOT. That will be difficult, I fear.

GLADYS. Not at all!

WYNCOT. But my duties in the case?

GLADYS. I absolve you from them.

WYNCOT. But can you?

GLADYS. Whether I can or not, I will! (*with petulant emphasis, accompanied with stamp of foot*)

WYNCOT. Ah!

GLADYS. (*haughtily*) Well, sir!—will you allow me to pass?

WYNCOT. (*after 'brief pause, stepping back, bowing, and removing his hat*) " When woman wills "——
GLADYS. (*sweeping past him, and turning up stage*) Farewell, sir!

(*Enter, suddenly, on path, up* R., CRAGIN. *As he appears, from behind a jutting rock about which the path turns, he catches sight of* WYNCOT *and* GLADYS, *halts instantly, and regards them, with evident satisfaction.* GLADYS, *at the same instant, observes* CRAGIN. *She, too, halts, and ejaculates:—*)

Oh!—A man!

WYNCOT. (*turning his head*) I perceive.

(CRAGIN, *turning, makes a quick exit, up* R., *as he came.*)

GLADYS. And now he has turned back.

(*In evident alarm, she retreats a step or two, toward* WYNCOT.)

How strangely he acted!
WYNCOT. Rather.
GLADYS. (*hesitatingly*) I think, sir—indeed, I am sure it was——
WYNCOT. My good friend, Cragin. Yes.
GLADYS. The man with whom you had a difficulty —yesterday. But you can hardly suppose——
WYNCOT. That he will annoy *you?* I trust not.
GLADYS. Or *you?*

(*An angry uproar, of many mingled voices, arises without—not far distant—off* R. U. E. *Fierce cries of* " Ay! " —" Ay! "—" Down wi' him! " GLADYS *starts, in affright, and draws nearer* WYNCOT.)

WYNCOT. (*again turning his head, and listening*) So! so!
GLADYS. Oh, sir!—what can it mean?
WYNCOT. Well, it means, I presume, Miss Wyncot, that the scout has reported to the main body—and that we may expect their attentions, soon.

(GLADYS *looks at him, in dismay.*)

In short, as you see, I have been much to blame. I have loitered here, chatting with you, when I should have been providing for your safety—with, or *without*, your consent. But, it is too late to retrieve the error—— (*looking about him, and moving* L.) Let me do what I can to find you a shelter from the consequences. (*at mouth of mine,* L. *front; lifting the vines which partially conceal it, and glancing in*) And this may serve the purpose. Unpleasant! But, for a time, at least——

GLADYS. And you would really have me believe there is danger?

WYNCOT. Of hard words—if nothing harder.

GLADYS. But why did you not tell me?

WYNCOT. Well!—I may have hinted at something of the sort.

GLADYS. Then I will stop and share it.

WYNCOT. Unfortunately you *must* stop—and share it, in a measure; but, unless you would double my difficulties, you will consent to be, for the present, invisible. (*again lifting the curtain of vines*) You will hardly demand a reason?

(*She stands, disturbed, and awed, but resentful, hesitating. The uproar, without, is again heard, nearer.*)

Immediately!—please!

GLADYS. (*her voice slightly tremulous*) Mr. Wyncot —if I have indeed been the means of— If I have thoughtlessly caused you——

WYNCOT. (*supplying the word*) "Trouble?"—How could you help it? Who can contend against the stars?

GLADYS. (*her resentment and spirit returning*) Then I will not ask your forgiveness; but will venture to remind you that it was not until your arrival that trouble came to this place. None the less, sir, I wish you, with all my heart, a speedy escape from it—and from one to whom, as you think, the stars are so evilly disposed.

(*With a haughty inclination of the head, she turns, and steps quickly within the mouth of the mine.* WYNCOT, *bowing, in response to her last words, lets fall the curtain of vines—through which, however, she is still visible.*)

WYNCOT. (*turning away*) What a vixen it is! And what a dolt am I! Ah, well——

CRAGIN. (*calling, without*) Come on!—ye cowardly curs!

WYNCOT. (*taking position, a step or two from mouth of mine, facing up* R., *and cutting the air with his light*

5

cane) Here, at least, is something that I can understand.

(Enter, on path up R., CRAGIN.*)*

CRAGIN. *(calling back)* Well! Are ye comin'?

(Enter, on path up R., SYKES.*)*

SYKES. *(joining* CRAGIN, *and calling back)* Ay! Come on! Here he bea!
MINERS. *(without, off* R. U. E., *shouting)* Come on! Come on! Down wi' him!

(Enter, on path up R., *a mob of miners, in working-dress—a number armed with clubs; others, with picks. Led by* CRAGIN *and* SYKES, *they rush down path, continuing to shout, and encourage one another with their cries—" Come on!"—" Down wi' him!"—The majority cross the bridge, and confront* WYNCOT. *A few stragglers stop on bridge, and on the farther bank of brook.* GLADYS, *just within the mouth of mine, is seen, through the foliage, to be listening intently, in tremulous suspense—bending forward, and striving to see, without being seen.)*

CRAGIN. *(in front of the crowd, as it halts)* Hold a bit, mates! Let *me* do the talkin'!

(Face to face with WYNCOT, *addressing him.)*

Well, my dandy pal!
WYNCOT. My good fellow!
CRAGIN. Again we meet.
WYNCOT. We do.
CRAGIN. And perhaps, in your opinion it's another occasion for takin' off caps?
WYNCOT. It may come to that.
CRAGIN. It may. But listen now to a few werry plain remarks! We've considered your offers of agreement——
WYNCOT. Yes.
CRAGIN. And they don't strike us favorable. *(to crowd)* Eh, mates?
SYKES *and* MINERS. No! No!
CRAGIN. And the question now is, which of us is likely to reconsider.
WYNCOT. That is the question. Will you allow me to speak?

CRAGIN. W'y, if it's to the point.

WYNCOT. It *shall* be—I promise you. And I must ask you all to listen. My friends——

CRAGIN. (*interrupting*) Ho! ho! His "friends!"

WYNCOT. Shall I be heard?

SYKES. Ay! Gi'e him his say!

WYNCOT. Thank you, my man! To be brief, then:—You have been notified that your wages have been increased, to the full extent of your request; and, in fact, that all your requests—but one—have been complied with. Yet you would now risk all that you have gained—and more; you would put in peril your entire livelihood, and the means on which it depends—only that this man, a stranger to you; and evidently new to your calling, may be placed above you, as "Overman."

CRAGIN. And wot know you of their "calling?"—or mine?—or w'ether I'm new or old to it?

WYNCOT. (*to the crowd*) But this is the case—as I have stated it? At all events, this man's appointment you insist upon?

CRAGIN. (*to the crowd*) Well?—Answer him!

SYKES. (*sullenly, but half-doubtingly*) Ay, sir!

MINERS. (*in the same manner*) Ay! Ay!

WYNCOT. (*taking paper from his pocket*) Then I must ask you to read with me this hand-bill—which the merest chance has thrown in my way, but which I think you may find interesting. (*reads*) "Escaped—from Dartmoor"——

CRAGIN. (*startled—interrupting*) Wot's that?

WYNCOT. (*reading, rapidly but forcefully*) "On the night of March 11th, a convict, under sentence for life; known by many aliases, and described"——

CRAGIN. (*again interrupting—violently*) Gammon! Wot sort of game are you givin' us? And who cares for that bloomin' rag? Come, stow it! (*striding forward, as if to seize paper*)

SYKES. (*restraining* CRAGIN) But, gi'e him his say!

WYNCOT. (*to* SYKES) Thank you, again! (*reads*) "And described as follows, to wit:—Height, five feet, ten inches"—— (*breaks off, and inspects* CRAGIN *from head to foot*)

CRAGIN. (*alarmed, but defiant*) Well—wot of it? Are you takin' my measure?

WYNCOT. (*reading*) "Hair, black; eyes, gray"—— (*again breaks off, and inspects* CRAGIN)

CRAGIN. (*mockingly*) "Hair, black! Eyes, gray!" Well—here you have 'em by the dozen. (*with wave of hand toward the miners, who are regarding him curi-*

ously and suspiciously—evidently comparing him with description)

WYNCOT. (*reading*) /' And "—last, but not least— " on the right shoulder, tattooed in blue and red, a gallows, with swinging noose." Cragin, you wear that mark.

CRAGIN. (*fiercely*) You lie!

WYNCOT. (*casting away the paper, and, at the same time, his cane*) You wear it. (*to the crowd*) And, look now, you that are honest men, while I show you——

CRAGIN. Wot? You fool! (*springing forward and aiming a savage blow at* WYNCOT)

(WYNCOT, *parrying the blow, grapples with* CRAGIN *in a fierce struggle.* GLADYS, *uttering an agonized cry, springs from the mouth of mine. The miners press forward toward the combatants.*)

SYKES. (*waving back the crowd, shouts:—*) Fair play!

(GLADYS, L., *with clasped hands, terror-stricken, watches the struggle, which is brief.* WYNCOT, *forcing* CRAGIN *back to* C., *suddenly lifts and throws him, over his* (WYNCOT'S) *right hip, bringing him to the ground between himself and* GLADYS; *and turning with him, and bending over him, as he falls, he tears the shirt from his shoulder, exposing the mark.*)

WYNCOT. (*to the crowd—indicating the mark*) Look!

(GLADYS *looks, and recoils.* SYKES *and his fellows all press forward to see.*)

SYKES. Ay! 'Tis so! A jail-bird!

MINERS. (*all—murmuring*) A jail-bird!

SYKES. A gallow's-bird! Down wi' him!

MINERS. (*in angry outburst*) Down wi' the jail-bird!

(WYNCOT, *half-assisting, half-dragging* CRAGIN *to his feet, hurls him* R.—*again bringing himself near to* GLADYS, *but facing* CRAGIN. CRAGIN, *rallying, surges forward, as if to renew the contest, but is restrained by* SYKES.)

SYKES. (*to* CRAGIN, *barring his advance*) Stand fast! (*to crowd—doffing and swinging his cap*) Hurrah, for the measter!

MINERS. (all, *doffing and swinging their caps—vociferously*) Hurrah, for the measter! Hurrah!

(WYNCOT, *turning, looks at* GLADYS. *She impulsively steps toward him, but checks herself, drops her face, and looks away.*)

Picture.

CURTAIN.

ACT IV.

SCENE.—*Drawing-room, Wyncot Lodge.* (*Set, as in Act 2.*) *Time, night. Chandelier and candelabra lighted. Fire in grate. View of garden, with moonlight effect, through window,* R. U. E., *oblique.*

(*Enter, at curtain,* EMILIA, *followed by* JAMES, *door* C. *She wears hat and wrap.*)

EMILIA. No!—thank you! But wait!
JAMES. Yes, miss.
EMILIA. And she is very much prostrated?
JAMES. Yes, miss. But I daresay, miss, you may see her.
EMILIA. Thank you—no! But wait!
JAMES. Yes, miss.
EMILIA. James, you may tell her—No!—Yes, you may tell her—that Miss Jekyll is here—to inquire after her health.
JAMES. Yes, miss.
EMILIA. You may tell her that—but nothing more.
JAMES. Yes, miss. (*correcting himself*) No, miss.
EMILIA. And then, if she likes—But that is all. Positively all!
JAMES. Yes, miss.

(*Exit* JAMES, *door* R. 2.)

EMILIA. And perhaps a deal too much! For it is certainly not my place—And if it were not for what has happened, and the fact that she has been punished—and has had time to be sorry——

(Enter James, *door* R. 2.)

James. I beg pardon, miss—she is just coming down.
Emilia. Oh!

(Enter Gladys, *door* R. 2. *She is in negligee, and hesitates, for an instant, at entrance, casting a quick, inquiring glance about the room.)*

Gladys. *(espying* Emilia) Emilia!

(After the first glance, the girls turn from each other. James *bows himself out, door* C. *The girls again face each other.)*

Emilia. Gladys!

(They rush into each other's embrace.)

Gladys. Now don't say a word about it!
Emilia. No! But you *do* forgive me?
Gladys. " Forgive " you?
Emilia. And what a fright you must have had!
Gladys. Well—perhaps. It wasn't so very jolly.
Emilia. No! I should say—And now—tell me! *(seating herself,* R. C. *front, and drawing* Gladys *down beside her)*
Gladys. What?
Emilia. Why, all about it—of course!
Gladys. And didn't I just ask you not to mention it?
Emilia. Oh! I thought you were speaking of something else.
Gladys. Besides, there is nothing to tell.
Emilia. Nothing?
Gladys. But what you have already heard. Mr. Wyncot had some trouble with the men. And I was there. And—and I got away—as you see.
Emilia. Gladys, what a girl you are!
Gladys. I knew you had heard it all.
Emilia. Why, if I had had such an adventure, it would have been my one consolation to think that I could tell of it afterward. But one thing you must admit.
Gladys. And what is that?
Emilia. That we made a mistake.
Gladys. In regard to what?

EMILIA. Well, in regard to Mr. Wyncot.

GLADYS. Now, Emilia!—Please——

EMILIA. But it can't be denied that he is not exactly what we thought him.

GLADYS. And if he isn't—is that any reason—Or perhaps you think, Emilia, that I am so fickle in my opinions that any little circumstance can change me?

EMILIA. Then you don't admire him?

GLADYS. (*rising*) "Admire him?" (*she paces* L.)

EMILIA. (*rising*) But that's no answer.

GLADYS. (*turning, facing her*) Then will this satisfy you?—Please never mention his name to me again. But *you* don't admire him?

EMILIA. (*joyfully*) Gladys, listen! It was my only fear that you might have changed your mind.

(*They again embrace, with mutual impulse, fervidly.*)

GLADYS. (*disengaging herself*) There! And now let us forget him!

EMILIA. If he will only allow us——

GLADYS. (*interrupting*) He will. Never fear! Indeed, I think I may assure you that he will give us but little more trouble.

EMILIA. Then you have not told me all!

GLADYS. (*warningly—checking her*) Emilia!

EMILIA. Oh, very well!

GLADYS. And now tell *me*:—have you heard from Richard?

EMILIA. Please never mention his name to me again! (*turning away*)

GLADYS. Oh!—Is it so bad as that?

EMILIA. (*again facing her*) No! It's so *good* as that! And let us forget *him*, too!

GLADYS. Do you mean it?—really?

EMILIA. Honors are easy, Gladys. They're a pretty pair. Let them go!

GLADYS. Oh, very well! But we have both had our experiences, Emilia.

EMILIA. Enough for a lifetime!

GLADYS. Quite enough!

EMILIA. (*half turning away, inspecting and stroking the glove on her hand*) Yes, I have no one to think of now, but papa. Poor papa!

GLADYS. After all, he was right—it would seem.

EMILIA. And he hasn't even said, "I told you so!" He has troubles of his own.

GLADYS. Indeed? But I daresay——

EMILIA. If you could only see him—and Mr. Job! They're to meet Mr. Wyncot, this evening, you know; and they're out there now in the moonlight, holding a conference. (*glancing toward window*)

GLADYS. Why, what about? Nothing serious, I hope.

(JEKYLL *and* JOB *suddenly appear in garden, just out-side window, walking slowly, in close converse. Each carries a huge ledger under his arm.* JEKYLL *is ges-ticulating violently.*)

EMILIA. (*espying them*) There they are!

GLADYS. (*approaching window, and gazing out*) Dear me! How excited your papa seems! And what are those enormous books they are carrying?

EMILIA. (*who has followed* GLADYS *to window—with vexation*) Well—they're the books of the estate—if you please.

GLADYS. (*enlightened*) Oh!

EMILIA. (*unlooping the window-curtains, preparatory to letting them fall*) You don't mind?

GLADYS. No! Certainly——

EMILIA. (*letting the curtains fall, shutting out view of garden*) I feel like saying what papa did.

GLADYS. About what?

EMILIA. The books. They've been worrying over them all afternoon—he, and Mr. Job—and I asked papa, at dinner, what the trouble was.

GLADYS. And what did he say?

EMILIA. He said, (*lowering her voice—impressively*) "Damn the books!"—And when papa goes to that length —you can imagine——

GLADYS. (*slightly shocked*) Really—yes!

EMILIA. And poor Mr. Job—though, of course, he doesn't swear——

(*Sound of door opening and shutting without.*)

Listen! They are coming in.

GLADYS. Oh! Then I mustn't be seen.

EMILIA. Why not?

GLADYS. (*indicating her gown*) In this?

EMILIA. But you are coming back?

GLADYS. No! You are coming up.

EMILIA. In a minute, then. I must speak with papa.

GLADYS. (*kissing her*) I shall expect you. Remember!

(Exit GLADYS, *hastily, door* R. 2.*)*

EMILIA. And then there's a chance that it may not be papa. Not that I care—particularly—to meet the other; but if he *should* happen to be about——

(Enter RICHARD, *door* C.*)*

And he happens. *(she turns from him quickly and gazes into space)*

RICHARD. Emilia! Miss Jekyll! Why do you shun me thus?

EMILIA. A pretty question, indeed!

RICHARD. A pertinent one, Emilia. Wherein have I offended?

EMILIA. *(scornfully)* You?——

RICHARD. Well—yes. You have heard, Emilia, that the strike has been summarily squelched?

EMILIA. Oh, you would like to change the subject.

RICHARD. And of the *coup d'etat,* if I may use the expression, by which this happy result has been brought about?

EMILIA. Much you had to do with it!

RICHARD. Well, Emilia, I was simply beyond the hill. It was merely the rising ground that intervened.

EMILIA. I'll warrant.

RICHARD. And if Mr. Wyncot had only waited——

EMILIA. Yes!—If he had——

RICHARD. I should have got there—in time. But all this is nothing. Surprising though it may seem, all that has occurred, Emilia, is as nothing, to that which will follow. But these are professional secrets. Emilia, you have suffered yourself to ossify your heart against me.

EMILIA. My heart is certainly hardened.

RICHARD. And ossification of the heart is a fatal disease.

EMILIA. It is? Well don't flatter yourself that I am thinking of dying.

RICHARD. No, Emilia, I do not. I am aware that you are a long liver. But, to approach the topic from another quarter:—you imagine, perhaps, that I am elated with my present prosperity?

EMILIA. I cannot imagine you a greater fool than before.

RICHARD. Thanks! But could you know! *(hand on breast)* Could you discern within!

EMILIA. Stuff!

RICHARD. "Stuff!" Unfeeling girl, perhaps within the hour, Othello's occupation will be gone.

EMILIA. Then Mr. Wyncot has discharged you, too?

RICHARD. Discharged me, "*too?*"

EMILIA. Well, you mean that, if you mean anything. And serves you right! When rogues fall out, honest people may get their dues.

RICHARD. Emilia!——

EMILIA. Miss Jekyll, if you please! And further, Mr. Jocelyn, I must beg that hereafter, when you succeed in surprising me alone——

RICHARD. Surprising you?

EMILIA. Yes, as on this occasion—you will pass quietly by, and spare me the necessity of avoiding you.

RICHARD. Emilia!——

EMILIA. Miss Jekyll, if you please!

RICHARD. Miss Jekyll, then!—You propose to pass judgment without hearing the defense?

EMILIA. The court has heard enough.

RICHARD. But the court is in error.

EMILIA. And the defendant is in contempt.

RICHARD. There *are* words—But I will not utter them.

EMILIA. No! I advise you not to.

RICHARD. For, though I should speak till doomsday, you would probably be speaking the day after.

(EMILIA *shrugs her shoulders, contemptuously.*)

I appeal, therefore, to the arbitration of Time.

EMILIA. Sir, make it Eternity, if you like!

RICHARD. (*bowing, sarcastically*) Just as you please, Miss Jekyll!

EMILIA. So be it, then!

RICHARD. So mote it be!

(*They turn in opposite directions:*—RICHARD *toward door,* L. 1.; EMILIA *toward door,* R. 2.)

EMILIA. (*turning toward him*) *Go* to your Mr. Wyncot!—and take a few more lessons in the art of "How to manage a woman."

RICHARD. (*turning—airily*) I will. Go you, to your *Miss* Wyncot!—and receive a little further instruction in the art of "How to distract a man."

EMILIA. Oh! Very good! But remember, Mr. Jocelyn, "they laugh best"——

RICHARD. (*interrupting*) "Who laugh last." Ha! ha!

(Exit EMILIA, *hastily, door* R. 2—*slamming the door be-*
hind her.)

And I laughed last. But oh!—misery!

*(*EMILIA *suddenly re-appears in doorway,* R. 2.*)*

EMILIA. *(simulating laughter—forced, like* RICHARD'S,
but louder and more mocking) Ha! ha!

(Again she̅ vanishes, and again the door slams.)

RICHARD. Ah—h!

(With a wild cry, he rushes off, door L. 1. *This door*
also slams. There follows a moment of silence. Then
the door, C., *opens slowly, and* JEKYLL, *carrying ledger*
under his arm, enters cautiously, peering about the
apartment.)

JEKYLL. *(speaking back, through door)* The coast is
clear.—Walk along! *Brace* hup, Mr. Job!

(Enter, door C., JOB, *timidly—under his arm, also, a*
ledger, of a size which taxes his strength.)
And keep your 'ead, sir!
JOB. *(removing his hat)* Dear, dear, sir!
JEKYLL. Well, sir! And now, sir—it is hunderstood?
JOB. W'y, sir, I trust——
JEKYLL. Let me recapitulate— *(depositing ledger, and*
hat, on table, L. C., *front)* Firstly:—the proper thing,
as I take it, is to offer our congratulations—on the
'appy termination of the strike.
JOB. Ay, sir! Firstly——
JEKYLL. That will soften, as it were, the hasperity of
the situation. See?
JOB. But secondly, sir?
JEKYLL. Ha! Secondly—*and thirdly*, Mr. Job—with
a proper amount of haudacity, you must place your de-
pendence on my natural sagacity. Eh?

(Slapping JOB *on the back. At the same instant, enter,*
door L. 1, WYNCOT, *followed by* RICHARD. JOB, *in his*
confusion, lets ledger fall to the floor.)

WYNCOT. Gentlemen! Good-evening!

*(*JEKYLL *bows, with stiff dignity.)*

JOB. Most kindly, sir—I'm sure!

(*Bowing, effusively, and backing, he stumbles on the fallen ledger.*)

JEKYLL. (*aside to* JOB—*supporting him*) 'Ang it! If you can't keep your 'ead, keep your feet, sir!
WYNCOT. You are prompt.
JEKYLL. (*picking up ledger*) Hit is our custom, sir.
WYNCOT. And you are evidently prepared to report.
JEKYLL. (*depositing the second ledger on table, with resounding thump*) We 'ave made some *little* preparation, sir.
WYNCOT. I see. Very good!
JEKYLL. (*striking attitude and beginning, oratorically*) Sir—on be'alf of myself, and colleague——
WYNCOT. (*interrupting*) Pardon me! (*strikes bell on table*) Before we begin——
JEKYLL. (*aside, to* JOB) There 'e goes again.

(*Enter* BUTTONS, *door* C.)

WYNCOT. Buttons!—say to Miss Wyncot, that I respectfully ask to see her—as soon as convenient.
BUTTONS. Yessir.
WYNCOT. You may go.

(*Exit* BUTTONS, *door* R. 2.)

However, we need not delay, on that account. You were about to say—— (*sits, L. of table, and waves* RICHARD *toward a chair—which the latter declines*) Be seated, Mr. Job.

(JOB *sits on edge of chair,* R.)

JEKYLL. Ha! Thank'ee, sir! I was about to say that we esteem it not only a duty, but a pleasure, to hexpress, sir, our gratification at the fortunate houtcome of your difficulties.
WYNCOT. You are very kind.
JEKYLL. In *hex*tricating yourself from a position so embarrassing, you 'ave shown, sir——
WYNCOT. (*interrupting*) My dear Mr. Jekyll! I can have no doubt of your high appreciation of my conduct; but my native modesty—Pray, spare me! And now, if you please, concerning the books——
JEKYLL. Ha! Very good, sir! The books—— (*aside*)

Bluffer number one, Mr. Job! (*to* WYNCOT) Concerning the books—as you say. Hexcuse me, sir!—my very
dear sir, hexcuse me, if I own to a feeling somewhat
akin to delicacy in broaching the subject, now to be considered. The books, sir—the books, as you be'old them—
(*pointing to the ledgers on table*) though nominally
under my charge, 'ave been, sir, for months, in a loca-
tion easy of haccess to a young man lately in my employ. (*looking hard at* RICHARD) The full significance
of this fact, I do not presume to state. But they exhibit,
sir, 'is 'and-writing, and they also exhibit—duty compels
me to add—some slight hirregularities.

WYNCOT. Ah?

JEKYLL. Now I would not be understood as 'inting
that these are the results of design. Far from it!
Rather would I regard them as mere hevidences of negli-
gence. But it is certainly to be regretted that they dis-
turb the balance, by some few pounds.

WYNCOT. So? By some few pounds?

JEKYLL. Well, by some few several pounds.

WYNCOT. Say, perhaps, fifty?

JEKYLL. Or a 'undred.

WYNCOT. Or possibly two hundred?

JEKYLL. Or two, and twenty.

WYNCOT. Ah!

JEKYLL. Hinsignificant though the sum may be, the
circumstance is, at least, unfortunate. But let us refrain
from haspersions! "To err is 'uman, to forgive, di-
vine!" (*stretching out his hands toward* RICHARD)

WYNCOT. But gently, Mr. Jekyll!

JEKYLL. Hexcuse me, sir, once more! Shall a mere
matter of some few several pounds be permitted to
darken the career of a generally well-meaning and has-
piring young man, whose greatest fault is per'aps 'is
lack of hintellect? No! On be'alf, sir, of myself and
colleague, I 'ere offer, as a sacrifice to the best hinter-
ests of society, our joint note of 'and, for the amount.

WYNCOT. Oh! And it is thus you propose to settle it?

JEKYLL. Mr. Job?

JOB. (*rising, anxiously, hand to ear*) Eh? As you
say, sir. (*falls back on chair*)

WYNCOT. And the entire deficit, you generously assume?

(JEKYLL *bows.*)

But the security?—Ah—to be sure! Mr. Job becomes
your security, and you become Mr. Job's?

JEKYLL. Jointly, sir.
JOB. (*rising, as before*) Most 'appy, sir, I'm sure. (*falls back, as before*)
WYNCOT. I perceive.—Well, Mr. Jocelyn, what say you?

(RICHARD *shrugs his shoulders.*)

You have no reply to make?
RICHARD. None, sir.
WYNCOT. Quite right! From you, at all events, no reply is required. (*rising*) And I must now inform you, Mr. Jekyll, that however much I might be disposed, personally, to accept this sacrifice, the affair is no longer under my control.
JEKYLL. (*anxiously*) 'Ow, sir?
JOB. (*rising—nervously*) Eh?
WYNCOT. This, while apparently a paradox, is readily explained. But the explanation requires the presence of yet other witnesses——

(*The door,* R. 2, *opens.*)

And, apropos, here are the ladies.

(*He advances toward door,* R. 2. JEKYLL *goes down* L. JOB *shuffles hastily across to* JEKYLL. *Enter. door* R. 2, GLADYS *and* EMILIA. GLADYS *is in evening dress.*)

Miss Wyncot! Miss Jekyl! You are quite in time. Pray be seated. (*offering chairs,* R., *which they accept*)
JOB. (*aside to* JEKYLL) 'Ow now, sir?
JEKYLL. (*aside to* JOB) Be quiet! Keep your 'ead, sir!
WYNCOT. (C.) Miss Wyncot, for again exercising my authority, to the extent of requesting an interview, I must tender an excuse, which you will grant, I am sure, upon the hearing, to be good and sufficient. Mr. Jekyll has just accounted to me for his stewardship of the estate. It now becomes my duty to account to you.
GLADYS. (*astonished*) To me, sir?
WYNCOT. You are surprised. I promise not to keep you long in suspense. And I beg, as a special favor, that you will, one and all, postpone any expressions of astonishment, or satisfaction, that may occur to you, in connection with the information which I am about to give you, till after the conclusion of my remarks. There will then be an abundant opportunity for an exchange of

sentiments—and I shall have been spared the interruptions.

(GLADYS *inclines her head.*)

JOB. (*aside to* JEKYLL) Eh?
JEKYLL. (*to* JOB) "Mum's the word."
JOB. (*to* WYNCOT) As you say, sir—I'm sure.
WYNCOT. Thanks! You are very kind.—At noon, to-day, Mr. Jocelyn entered my employ. The amount of labor which he has since performed is certainly remarkable;—and the extent of his discoveries not less so. In assorting and arranging my late uncle's papers—at many of which I had not even glanced—he has chanced upon one, at least, of very grave importance. In bringing it to light, he has sacrificed, virtually, the position which I had given him, and I trust, Miss Wyncot, that you, to whose benefit the discovery inures, will see to it that he is not the loser by his faithfulness.

(*He holds toward* JEKYLL *an open document, which he has carried, since entering, in his hand.*)

Mr. Jekyll, do you know this signature?

(JEKYLL *offers to take paper, but is prevented by* WYNCOT.)

Pardon me!
JEKYLL. (*inspecting paper in* WYNCOT'S *hand*) I do, sir.
WYNCOT. And it is that of my late uncle?
JEKYLL. It is—hif I ever saw it.
WYNCOT. That is quite sufficient. The document to which it is attached—and the body of which, you will observe, is in the same handwriting— (*displaying it*) is, if not in form, at least in effect, a will.
JEKYLL. (*astounded*) A will?
WYNCOT. A will. It is of later date than that by which I inherit—or was supposed to inherit—and it confers upon you, Miss Wyncot, the sum total of the property of which the testator died possessed. (*he tenders* GLADYS *the document*)
GLADYS. (*rising—astonished, and incredulous*) Mr. Wyncot! (*shrinking back, she declines to take the paper*)
WYNCOT. Still further—it leaves you free to select your own guardian, and I congratulate you, Miss Wyncot—and may also be allowed to congratulate myself—

upon this happy release from a relationship, which was beginning to prove annoying to us both.

(*With an impulsive movement, she seizes the paper, glances at it, and crushing it in her hand, gazes on* WYNCOT. EMILIA, *in joyous surprise and agitation, rises, steps to* GLADYS' *side, and puts an arm about her.*)

EMILIA. Gladys!
JEKYLL. (*puffing with elation*) Well, sir! Well, sir!
JOB. (*gasping, with relief*) Dear, dear, sir!
WYNCOT. One moment!—Having passed from the position of inspector, I now ask to be inspected. Mr. Jocelyn has prepared, at my request, a report of my brief incumbency.

(RICHARD *produces a folded document, and unfolds it.* WYNCOT *addresses* GLADYS.)

Will you kindly empower Mr. Jekyll to overlook that report?
GLADYS. (*in agitation—turning away*) Oh, sir!——
WYNCOT. (*consulting watch*) It is now half-past eight. The London train is due at half-past nine. If, within that time——

(GLADYS, *her face still averted, makes an impatient gesture.*)

Ah! You are more than kind. (*he strikes bell, on table*) And meanwhile I have a few letters to write. You will excuse me?

(*Enter* BUTTONS, *door* C., *his hands behind him.*)

Buttons!
BUTTONS. Yessir.
WYNCOT. Order the trap. (*to* GLADYS—*apologetically*) If I may now presume to give an order?—the last upon which I shall venture, here.

(GLADYS *casts a quick glance toward him, and again turns away, with look and gesture at once indignant and distressed.* WYNCOT *turns to the waiting* BUTTONS.)

The trap, Buttons!
BUTTONS. Yessir.

(He starts backward, toward door, c.)

WYNCOT.   And—Stop!

(BUTTONS *halts.*)

I should like to take with me some souvenir of the place, which has afforded me so many interesting—if not always pleasant—experiences; and I have rather taken a fancy to *you*. If you like my service, prepare to accompany me.

BUTTONS.   Yessir.   W'ere to, sir?

WYNCOT.   To India.

(BUTTONS' *mouth flies open, from amazement, and a pasty, which he has been concealing behind him, falls from his hands to the floor.*)

Ladies!   Gentlemen!   (*bowing right and left*) I shall be in the library, if wanted.

(*Exit* WYNCOT, *door, L. 1.*)

BUTTONS.   Mamma!   (*shouting the word, he seizes up the pasty, and rushes off, door, c.*)

JEKYLL.   (*slapping* JOB *on the back*) Well, sir!   Well, sir!

EMILIA.   Gladys!   Why don't you speak?

GLADYS.   Oh!—But *can* it be true, Mr. Jekyll?   (*extending the paper toward him*)

JEKYLL.   (*taking paper*) "True," miss?   Well, as I've said, I can take my hoath to the signature.   And—ha!—yes!—'ere you 'ave it.   (*reads from paper*) "I give and bequeath "——

(GLADYS *snatches the paper from his hand.*)

GLADYS.   Emilia!   (*she turns, and falling on* EMILIA's *shoulder, hides her face*)

JEKYLL.   Ah, wot a man was 'e, Mr. Job, who penned those lines!

JOB.   (*with fervor*) A good man, sir—truly!

JEKYLL.   A great man, sir!—But wot did I 'ear about certain accounts?

RICHARD.   They are ready, sir.   Will you inspect them?

6

JEKYLL. (*to* JOB, *nudging him*) Will we? Well—
possibly——
GLADYS. (*turning quickly*) But not here, please!
JEKYLL. And w'ere then, miss?
GLADYS. Oh, any where!—so that you leave us alone!
EMILIA. Yes, papa, for goodness' sake—— (*to*
GLADYS) Why not the smoking-room?
GLADYS. (*impatiently*) Yes, yes!
EMILIA. You hear, papa? In the smoking-room!
JEKYLL. (*to* RICHARD) Lead the way, young man!
Walk along! Mr. Job!—haccept my arm, sir!
JOB. (*taking* JEKYLL's *arm*) Dear, dear, sir. Wot a
deliverance!
JEKYLL. (*to* JOB) "Virtue," Mr. Job—gets there—hin
time!

(*Exit* RICHARD, *door* C. *Exeunt* JEKYLL *and* JOB, *arm in
arm, immediately following* RICHARD.)

EMILIA. And now—Gladys! Let me look at you! It
is like a scene from a play. (*turning the unwilling*
GLADYS *about and looking into her face*) Why, you are
positively crying!
GLADYS. "Crying?"
EMILIA. Yes, you are. Gladys! what ails you?
GLADYS. (*pacing the floor*) Emilia—I believe that I
am crazy.
EMILIA. Or are certainly going to be. Why, I sup-
posed that you would be wild with delight.
GLADYS. "Delight?" At what?
EMILIA. "At what?"
GLADYS. At being openly insulted? At being treated
as though I were a mere——
EMILIA. Well? A mere heiress?
GLADYS. Emilia, will you hold your tongue?
EMILIA. Gladys——
GLADYS. Why, it is as plain as day! He gives it to
me. He simply wishes to get away.
EMILIA. Can you suspect——
GLADYS. "Suspect?"—Such a story! After your papa
had examined all the papers!
EMILIA. That is true. But Richard——
GLADYS. Well—couldn't Richard have been pur-
chased?
EMILIA. Gladys——
GLADYS. Now we will not discuss that question. But
nothing can convince me that it is not a shameful in-

vention. (*glancing at paper, which she holds folded in her hand*)

EMILIA. (*referring to paper*) You might tell by looking—I should think.

GLADYS. (*thrusting the paper into her bosom*) And then, his manner! To surrender it all, with such an air! To congratulate himself!—Did you hear him? And to allow no one a chance to reply! Emilia, he is behind that door. I must see him.

EMILIA. You *are* crazy.

GLADYS. And you have only to knock——

EMILIA. I? Not for the crown jewels!

GLADYS. Emilia, did you ever know me to determine to do a thing, and not do it?

EMILIA. No! Never!

GLADYS. Well then, when I tell you that I *will* see him——

EMILIA. For goodness' sake! Let me ring for Buttons!

GLADYS. Buttons? That prying young imp!

EMILIA. James, then—

GLADYS. James? I don't wish to see James.

EMILIA. Well, you needn't expect *me* to go near that door—and that I tell you plainly. For I would as soon walk into Bluebeard's closet.

GLADYS. Then I will do it, myself.

EMILIA. You won't!

GLADYS. Emilia, you may go, or stay; but knock at that door I certainly will——

EMILIA. Gladys!

GLADYS. (*crossing toward door, L. 1*) And that, this minute!

EMILIA. (*in horror*) Oh! (*she runs out, hastily, door c.*)

GLADYS. (*pausing, near door, L. 1*) But what will he think? And what can I say? If he were not so hatefully polite!—and so abominally self-sufficient! Oh!—why did he come here? I was happy enough till I saw him. I *hate* him—and I'll tell him so. (*moves again toward door, L. 1. Again pauses*) But that is probably just what he wishes to hear. (*looks behind her—calls faintly*) Emilia!—She'll laugh at me now, if I don't. (*goes quickly up to door, c., looks out, draws a disappointed breath, closes the door, carefully, and again turns down stage*) There is no one whom I can trust. No one! Oh, what shall I do? I wish the room were two stories from the ground. I'd jump from the window. (*turning impulsively, toward window, up R.*)

(CRAGIN *steps from behind curtains of window—in his hand a pistol, which he levels at* GLADYS. *Note:—Both he and* GLADYS, *throughout the ensuing scene, speak in repressed and constrained tones.*)

CRAGIN. I'll save you the trouble, miss—if you open your mouth or so much as wink an eyelid. Sit down!

(GLADYS *sinks into chair.*)

That's it. Now be sensible.

GLADYS. (*faintly*) What do you want, sir?

CRAGIN. Not you! I think I understood you that Mr. Wyncot is near by.

GLADYS. And what can you want with Mr. Wyncot?

CRAGIN. You're curious. But I don't mind telling you. I want to settle a score.

GLADYS. Oh, sir——

CRAGIN. (*shaking pistol, ominously*) And here's the coin ready.

GLADYS. (*half rising*) And you think that I will permit——

CRAGIN. And how do you hope to hinder me? By screamin'? But he'll be the first to come. And if once he crosses that doorway—— (*looking toward door,* I. 1)

GLADYS. (*sinking back*) Oh!

CRAGIN. No—you've thought better of it. That's right! Only just you sit still! (*he makes movement to cross toward door,* L. 1)

GLADYS. (*detaining him, with appealing gesture*) But why should you wish to harm him?

CRAGIN. Oh, come now, miss!

GLADYS. At least he permitted you to escape.

CRAGIN. "Escape?" Sure enough! He didn't trouble himself to haul me afore the beak. He left that to others. But just the same, I'm marked—and I'm followed. (*he moves toward* L.)

GLADYS. Oh, not yet, sir! Not yet! Will nothing tempt you? Money——

CRAGIN. "Money?" Bah!

GLADYS. My jewelry—you shall have it all.

CRAGIN. In few words, miss, you talk against the wind. Wot's money—or wot's jewels—to him that can't even get away with his precious bones?

GLADYS. But if you *could* get away?

CRAGIN. Ah! If I could!

GLADYS. Oh, sir, I beg of you—I implore you to listen. A vessel will cross the Channel, to-night—from the Cove, near-by—on the next tide. If you were once on board who would think of searching for you there? And perhaps in some foreign land, you might yet lead a better and a happier life. Oh, if you will only hear me!

CRAGIN. Hold a bit, miss! If I were aboard! But how am I to get aboard?

GLADYS. But if I can find you a way?

CRAGIN. Tell me the way, and I'll tell you wot I think of it.—But wot know you of the craft in the Cove?—or w'ere they are bound for?

GLADYS. The ship is the "Swallow." Mr. Wyncot has chartered it. You shall have an order——

CRAGIN. "An order?"

GLADYS. Directing the master to receive you as a passenger, without question, and without price.

CRAGIN. And who's to write that order?

(GLADYS *glances toward door*, L. 1. CRAGIN'S *glance follows hers.*)

Not he?

GLADYS. (*firmly*) Yes!—he!

CRAGIN. You're a-gammonin' me.

GLADYS. I promise it. And, if I fail, you shall kill me, instead.

CRAGIN. (*after slight pause—regarding her*) Look'ee, miss! You love him.

(GLADYS *drops her face.*)

That's wot it means. But tastes will differ. Your bribe is worth considerin'.

GLADYS. (*eagerly*) And you accept it?

(CRAGIN *gazes at her, for an instant, searchingly—then, half turning away, draws a deep breath, passing his hand across his brows.* GLADYS *springs to her feet.*)

God will bless you!

CRAGIN. (*seizing her by the wrist*) But steady! Did I say yes?

GLADYS. Your heart said it. And Oh, surely, freedom and safety are better than revenge.

CRAGIN. Mayhap they are, miss! And I guess your game—but how am I to know it'll win? Come! It's a bargain—*providin'*—it's here, and now, you play your hand.

GLADYS. (*faintly*) Here?

CRAGIN. Understand! I've no great faith; and I take no extra chances. But here, at worst, I'll have you in sight—— (*with glance toward window and flourish of pistol*) and him in reach. Is it agreed, miss?

(GLADYS *sinks helplessly back into chair.*)

Then sit you there till the game is called! And see that you play me fair! (*he crosses toward door,* L. 1)
GLADYS. (*half-rising*) But you are not going——
CRAGIN. (*turning quickly and presenting pistol*) Sit down!

(GLADYS *sinks back, as before.*)

I'm goin' to do the knockin' for you, miss—and you've kindly told me he's "behind that door."

(GLADYS *moans and wrings her hands.*)

Steady now! (*he raps on door,* L. 1, *and bending his ear toward it, listens intently*)
GLADYS. (*also listening—after a moment, breathlessly*) But quick! He is coming!
CRAGIN. (*shaking his head, and lifting his hand, warningly*) Steady! (*he raps again—louder*)
GLADYS. Oh, Heaven! (*suddenly, in agonized whisper—half-rising*) Quick! Quick! He is here!
CRAGIN. (*retreating, backward, toward window*) Quiet, miss! Quiet, and steady! And keep you out of range!

(GLADYS, *leaning forward, in an agony of suspense, her hands clutching the arms of chair, watches alternately* CRAGIN'S *retreat and the door,* L. 1. CRAGIN *disappears behind curtains of window, up* R. *At the same instant,* WYNCOT *appears in doorway,* L. 1.)

GLADYS. (*springing erect, with half-stifled cry*) Ah!
WYNCOT. (*pausing in doorway*) Miss Wyncot!

(*She sways and sinks back into chair.* WYNCOT *hastens to her side.*)

You are ill!
GLADYS. (*rallying, instantly*) No! no! It is nothing.
WYNCOT. "Nothing?" It was you that knocked?

(She evades reply—glancing toward window.)

But surely you are ill. You are trembling. Something has frightened you. *(he moves, as if to cross toward window)*

GLADYS. *(desperately—rising, and intercepting him)* No! Will you not believe me? I wished to see you—to speak with you. But not of myself!

WYNCOT. Of whom, then?

GLADYS. *(half-turning away)* How shall I tell you?

WYNCOT. Well! I listen.

GLADYS. *(suddenly facing him, with the courage of desperation)* Of one who has wronged you. Of the convict.

WYNCOT. *(astounded)* "The convict?"

GLADYS. Oh, sir, to a fallen foe—one so friendless, and outcast—can you not well afford to be merciful? Be more than merciful!—be generous! Whatever he may have been, or done, has he not been sufficiently punished?

WYNCOT. My dear Miss Wyncot——

GLADYS. *(interrupting)* You must not think it strange! I have a reason—Oh, trust me, sir!—and answer! Or, rather, do not answer, but do what I bid you—and ask me nothing!

WYNCOT. But pardon me! I am compelled to think it strange—that you should appeal to *me*, on *his* behalf! Surely *I* have shown no evidence of a disposition to persecute him. And why such interest upon your part?

GLADYS. *(in agony, with furtive glance toward window)* You must not question—but *trust* me!—for your *own* sake! Oh, I entreat you——

WYNCOT. For my own sake! He has threatened my life. Is that a reason why I should be kind to him?—Or, can it be that that commends him to you?

(He speaks with bitterness, but half-concealed. GLADYS utters a hopeless cry, and breaks into convulsive sobbing, covering her face with her hands. WYNCOT impulsively moves toward her, speaking contritely:—)

Forgive me!

GLADYS. *(shrinking back and repelling him)* No! no! Do not come near me!

WYNCOT. That was the speech of a brute. I humbly beg you to forget it. And to atone for it, I will do whatever you wish.

GLADYS. *(eagerly)* You promise?

WYNCOT. Either with, or without an explanation.

GLADYS. Quick, then! Sit there—and write! (*urging him toward table*, L.)

WYNCOT. (*approaching table and glancing over it*) But the materials! (*turning, he looks toward escritoire, up* R.)

GLADYS. (*quickly*) I will fetch them. (*she hastens to escritoire, and procures writing materials*)

WYNCOT. (*aside*) Mystery!—thy name is woman.

GLADYS. (*returning with pen, ink and paper, which she places on table*) Now! Oh, make haste! Write!

WYNCOT. (*seating himself at table and taking pen*) Dictate!

GLADYS. (*dictating*) To the master of the "Swallow"——

WYNCOT. (*glances up at her—then writes*) "To the master of the ' Swallow ' "——

GLADYS. (*dictating*) You will receive the bearer—as a passenger—— (*she breaks off for a moment, while* WYNCOT *writes*) without charge—to your destination.

WYNCOT. (*looking up*) That is to say, Bremenhaven.

GLADYS. (*clasping her hands*) Write!

(WYNCOT *writes. She again dictates.*)

And you will ask him no questions.

WYNCOT. (*finishing*) It is written.

GLADYS. But sign it.

WYNCOT. You forget. I have no longer the authority——

GLADYS. (*in frantic impatience*) Oh, sign! For to-night, at least, who will question——

WYNCOT. (*signing*) It is signed. (*he rises, gives her the paper, and stands, for a moment, regarding her*) And that is all? I may go now?

GLADYS. (*falteringly*) Y-yes!

WYNCOT. (*not without bitterness*) Thank you! I *did* hope—when I learned that it was you who knocked at my door—But, to be sure, I had no right to hope. Come, then!—since all our accounts are closed—we may part as friends? Or, at least, not quite as enemies? (*he offers his hand. She takes it, hesitatingly*) That was a very feeble grasp. You can do no better?

GLADYS. (*faintly—withdrawing her hand*) Go!

WYNCOT. (*turning toward door*, L. 1) Farewell! (*he suddenly pauses and turns again toward her*) But stay! "Receive the bearer." But how do you propose to get that paper into Cragin's hands?

GLADYS. (*all her terrors returning*) You must not ask!

WYNCOT. I must. And I must have an answer.

GLADYS. (*wildly*) Oh, go! Go!

WYNCOT. Surely you will not meet him? Or, if so, where?

GLADYS. Go! Have you not promised?

WYNCOT. (*advancing toward her*) It is night; you cannot go to him. Will he dare come to you?

GLADYS. (*retreating before him, and repelling him, with frantic gestures*) For your life's sake! Go!

WYNCOT. (*advancing and speaking rapidly*) You expect him! He is here! He is behind those curtains!

(*He springs toward window, up R. GLADYS, with a shriek, throws her arms about him, stopping his progress. CRAGIN steps from behind curtains of window, throwing up his hands, which are empty. WYNCOT, with self-accusation, comments:—*)

As I might have guessed!

CRAGIN. Don't be alarmed, sir! Don't be alarmed, miss! It's true, as you see, I am here. And, moreover, it's true, sir, I came to kill you—and for nothing else——

GLADYS. (*to WYNCOT—her arms still enclasping him*) Don't speak!

CRAGIN. But, like many another, I've listened to the wheedling of a woman's tongue. And so, if you please, I'll take my ticket-of-leave. (*he advances a step, extending his hand for the order, which GLADYS holds*)

WYNCOT. Will you?

GLADYS. Yes! Yes! He shall have it.

(*She attempts to pass the order to CRAGIN. WYNCOT prevents her—seizing her wrist.*)

Oh! In Heaven's name——

CRAGIN. (*alarmed, drawing back*) Have a care, sir! (*his hand goes to his pocket, and he half-draws forth pistol*)

WYNCOT. (*in low tones, to GLADYS, striving, though gently, to put her aside*) Why have you done this? Give it me! Leave the room!

GLADYS. (*clinging to him, and maintaining her position between him and CRAGIN*) I will not.

CRAGIN. (*surlily and threateningly*) Come! Make haste, sir! Unless you'd prefer——

WYNCOT. (*suddenly seizing the order from* GLADYS' *hand, thrusting her behind him, and facing* CRAGIN) I *would*——

(GLADYS, *shrieking, retains her clutch on* WYNCOT'S *arm.* CRAGIN, *whipping the pistol from his pocket, levels it at* WYNCOT. WYNCOT *continues, without pause.*)

I would *very much* prefer to make my own bargains. Oh, you coward! To take such advantage! To compel a woman to beg for you what you could never have won——

GLADYS. (*interrupting*) It is not true! He did not compel me. He forbade me to speak—to warn you. But he had pity;—and Oh, will you have less?

(WYNCOT, *turning his head, looks into* GLADYS' *face. Still clinging to him, she averts her gaze.*)

CRAGIN. (*lowering his pistol*) Well! You hear, sir? And you understand? It's little she cares for the poor devil of a "lifer," or wot becomes of *him.* And why should *you* care—after this?

(WYNCOT, *suddenly, without changing position, extends the order to* CRAGIN. CRAGIN, *stepping forward, takes it, with bowed head, but gruffly:*—)

Thank'ee, sir!

WYNCOT. No thanks! Have you money? You will need it. (*he tosses purse to* CRAGIN)

CRAGIN. (*amazed—picking up purse*) Wot? You give me this?

WYNCOT. Go!—while the way is open.

CRAGIN. (*affected*) But you'll allow me, sir!—It isn't much you can expect from one of my sort, in the way of gratefulness—and, least of all, a sermon. But wot I have to offer, if you'll hear it, sir, and give me credit——

WYNCOT. (*interrupting*) Be brief!

CRAGIN. Twenty years ago, this night, my sweetheart and I, we stood together on the bridge, at Stamford. Our pride had come between us. We loved each other, but neither would be the first to speak. And so, for the lack of a word, we parted—I, to the hulks—she, to the Stamford churchyard. You draws your own moral. Good-night!

(*Exit* Cragin, *through window.* Gladys *sinks into chair,* l., *leaning and looking away from* Wyncot, *who stands, regarding her, with evident emotion.*)

Wyncot. (*after brief pause*) And what moral, Gladys, shall *we* draw?

(*He moves toward her. She throws her arms across the arm of chair, and lowers and hides her face.*)

Forgive me! I presume, perhaps, upon your kindness. It may be that to one of us, only, does the poor fellow's sermon appeal—or apply;—but speak, now, I must, and make my confession. Yes!—humbly, and contritely, let me own it!—all my criticism of you—all the light and foolish speeches, in which I have so lightly commented upon you, with seeming disfavor, or indifference, have been the paltriest of shams, the most pitiful of pretences. One and all, they have had but one motive—to conceal a feeling which I dared not acknowledge, even to myself—fearing for my own peace of mind.

(*On the last phrase he again moves a step toward her. In extreme agitation, she rises, and retreats,* l., *still facing away from him.*)

And now—though all this you must have known—at least we shall not part " for lack of a word."—Well! I have spoken.

(*She turns, as if about to address him; attempts to speak, but fails; and crossing rapidly to fireplace,* r. 1, *leans against the mantel, and again conceals her face.* Wyncot, *motionless, follows her with his eyes, sadly.*)

And am answered. Even so! Here, no reconciliation is possible. (*a tinge of bitterness again creeps into his tone*) Ah, well! your revenge is complete. You are freed from your fetters; you have succeeded to your rights; and now, at the last, you have saved my life— only to show me its emptiness, and worthlessness. Surely I may now, with confidence, and in all sincerity, wish you happiness.

Gladys. (*turning on him*) And you can think so meanly of me? At least, do me the justice to believe that *this* does not add to my happiness. (*impetuously taking the will from her bosom, and extending it toward him*)

WYNCOT. (*wonderingly—taking the will*) This?

GLADYS. How could you think to impose upon me with such a transparent—— (*with a shrug of the shoulders, she breaks off and turns away*)

WYNCOT. What? Surely you do not question its genuineness? But look! Convince yourself! You should know the handwriting. (*opening the paper and holding it toward her*) And, as to its meaning, it is all that I have claimed for it.

GLADYS. (*speaking over her shoulder—in petulant remonstrance*) Then why did you not conceal it?—or destroy it? Why should you throw upon me the burdens which you find too heavy, or too troublesome to bear? (*suddenly turns and seizes the paper from his hand*) Ah! confess!—there is but *one* burden that really oppresses you.

WYNCOT. (*more and more perplexed*) Miss Wyncot——

GLADYS. You have named it. And only to rid yourself of that, you would make this sacrifice.

WYNCOT. Can you believe——

GLADYS. (*impetuously, interrupting*) And can *you* believe that I will consent to it?—or that I will accept such a charity at your hands? I asked you, it is true, to find—for both of us—some way of escape;—but is this the best that you can devise?

WYNCOT. (*mystified, but mildly protesting*) Surely——

GLADYS. (*interrupting*) Yes! surely there is a better way. (*turns suddenly toward grate, R. 1, and casts the will into the fire*) It is *I* who will go—and as poor as I came.

WYNCOT. (*springing forward to prevent her*) Ah! Stop! Do you know what you do?

GLADYS. (*barring his way*) I know—and I forbid you to touch it!

WYNCOT. (*seeking to rescue the will*) But you must not! You shall not!——

GLADYS. (*resolutely opposing him.*) If you speak the truth, till that burns I am the mistress here.

WYNCOT. (*staggered*) Gladys!

GLADYS. And whatever the truth may be——

WYNCOT. Ah! (*with another effort to reach the grate*)

(*The will, in the meantime, has vanished in the flames.*)

GLADYS. Too late! It is gone. And now you may do what you will with your own!

(*She turns toward door, up* C. WYNCOT *catches her about the waist. She struggles, feebly, to escape.*)

WYNCOT. And this is what I would do—*with my own.* (*he draws her head down upon his shoulder*) Yes! And who shall gainsay me? (*he kisses her—without protest*)

(BUTTONS *suddenly thrusts in his head, door* C., *gazes for a moment, wild-eyed, and vanishes, leaving the door open behind him.*)

BUTTONS. (*calling as he goes:—*) Mamma!
WYNCOT. (*whirling toward the vanishing* BUTTONS) You young jackanapes! (*to* GLADYS) Never mind! Love, like murder, " will out "—and the sooner the better! (*glancing out through door*, C.) Here they come.

(GLADYS *goes* L., *and stands beside table.* WYNCOT *remains* R. *Enter, door* C., JEKYLL *and* JOB, *followed immediately by* RICHARD.)

JEKYLL. (*entering*) Ha! Well, sir!
WYNCOT. Walk in, Mr. Jekyll! You are waited for. You have examined the report?
JEKYLL. We 'ave, sir; and we find it in the main satisfactory.
WYNCOT. (*bowing*) Thanks!

(*Enter* EMILIA, *hesitatingly, door* C. GLADYS, *observing her, signals her, and, while* JEKYLL *is delivering the ensuing speech, she moves down, unobtrusively,* L. *of table, and joins* GLADYS, L. *front.*)

JEKYLL. (*to* WYNCOT) But excuse me, sir! There's one little matter that you seem to 'ave overlooked. (*he turns to* GLADYS) Your property, miss, as you probably know, 'as suffered damage—'eavy damage—in the course of recent events; and it's our opinion, jointly and severally, (*referring to* JOB) that the party responsible for the aforesaid events, is liable for the cost of repairs.
GLADYS. Meaning Mr. Wyncot?

(JEKYLL *bows assent.*)

But to *whom* is he liable? Certainly not to me. For I have just destroyed my only evidence of title.
JEKYLL. (*incredulously*) Wot?
GLADYS. You will find the ashes in the grate.

Job. (*to* Jekyll, *in anxious bewilderment*) Eh? Mr. Jekyll?

(Jekyll *distractedly mops his forehead.*)

Emilia. (*to* Gladys, *excitedly, and unbelievingly— half-aside*) · Gladys! Can it be?
Wyncot. Strange!—but true! And the explanation is still more strange. (*crossing to* Gladys *and* Emilia, *as he speaks, and addressing the latter:—*) Rashly, as you may think, I fear, yet hoping for your approval, Miss Jekyll, she kindly accepts me as guardian for life.

(*He takes* Gladys' *hand, and lifts it to his lips.* Emilia *turns, as if to fly.* Wyncot *adds, quickly:—*)

Stop! Don't go!

(Gladys *puts her arm about* Emilia, *detaining her.* Richard *exhibits pleased surprise, and glances, longingly and reproachfully, toward* Emilia. Jekyll *narrowly escapes collapse, and turns to the equally dismayed* Job.)

Jekyll. (*throwing up his hands*) "Settled—out of court!"
Wyncot. And now, Mr. Jekyll, another little matter! We are both, it would appear, in debt to the estate. But may not the accounts be allowed to offset each other?
Jekyll. (*perplexed, but hopeful*) 'Ow, sir?
Wyncot. I now propose such an adjustment—on condition—— (*he turns to* Richard, *and extends his hand*) Mr. Jocelyn!
Richard. (*wonderingly, advancing, and giving his hand to* Wyncot) Mr. Wyncot!
Wyncot. (*holding* Richard's *hand, and turning to* Emilia) Miss Jekyll! Allow me! Your hand, if you please!

(*He possesses himself of* Emilia's *hand, and leads the pair toward* Jekyll—Emilia *making a show of resistance.*)

On condition, my dear Mr. Jekyll, that you now bestow on these two most worthy, and mutually-devoted young people, your fatherly blessing. .

(*To* EMILIA, *who further resists.*)

Eh? Come! come!

(*He places her hand, willy nilly, in that of* RICHARD—
on whom, however, she refuses to look.)

RICHARD. (*appealingly*) Emilia! Last call!

(*She turns suddenly, with movement as if about to embrace* RICHARD; *but refrains, and dragging* RICHARD
with her, falls on her knee, before JEKYLL. RICHARD
*plumps down beside her, on both knees, and bows his
head.*)

EMILIA. Papa!
JEKYLL. (*mopping his forehead, and glancing down
on* RICHARD) Well, sir! Well, sir! This is a surprise.
EMILIA. (*reproachfully*) Oh, papa!
JEKYLL. A shock, as I may say. But wot 'ave I al-
ways said, Mr. Job? (*extending his hand over* RICH-
ARD'S *head, and turning to* JOB) A worthy young man!
JOB. A good man, sir!
JEKYLL. (*to* RICHARD, *with beneficent gesture*) Take
'er! Be 'appy!

(RICHARD *and* EMILIA *rise quickly, and* RICHARD, *to his
partner's great horrification, implants an audible kiss
on her cheek.*)

WYNCOT. (*with the air of one who has arrived at the
happy termination of trouble*) And so, we may trust——

(*Enter, door* R. 2, MRS. PRINGLE, *leading* BUTTONS. WYN-
COT, *observing her, checks himself, and exclaims with
deploring gesture.*)
Ah! Not yet!
MRS. P. (*to* WYNCOT) Which I 'opes, sir——
WYNCOT. (*seeking to silence her*) My dear Mrs.
Pringle——
MRS. P. (*not to be silenced*) Which I 'opes, sir, that
I'm still on *terry firmus;* though I 'ave my doubts, I
confess, along of such carryin's—and goin's-on. But of
all things, as I must say——
WYNCOT. Will you allow me——
MRS. P. As I must say, sir—a lone woman!—and a
lorn woman!—and with never a chick nor a child but

one!—and 'im that delikit and sensytive, as could scarce abear a 'arsh word, or so much as the wind that blows!— (*looking down on* BUTTONS) and now to 'ave 'im torn from my harms!

WYNCOT. (*once more vainly attempting a diversion*) But, madam——

MRS. P. And of all places on this mortal earth, for a growin' boy—if it's *on* the earth, which I 'ave my doubts—save and deliver us, or *me*, leastwise, from Hinjy!—w'ere they stand, as I'm told, with their 'eads down, bein' quite rewersed——

(WYNCOT *turns, helplessly and appealingly, to* JEKYLL.)

JEKYLL. (*stepping in front of* MRS. P.) Woman!—"Get thee to a nunnery!" W'y all this lamentation? No one would deprive you of Young 'Opeful.

MRS. P. No?

JEKYLL. No! 'Eaven forbid! And no one is going away. Hon the contrary, the demand, ma'am, is not for 'andkerchiefs, but horange-blossoms.

MRS. P. Lor', sir!

JEKYLL. (*to the others*) Do I correctly hexpress myself?

WYNCOT. Gladys! (*he again lifts her hand to his lips*)

RICHARD. Emilia! (*he embraces her*)

JEKYLL. Mr. Job! (*he draws* JOB's *arm through his own, smiling down upon him beamingly*)

MRS. P. (*opening her arms to* BUTTONS) Buttons!

BUTTONS. (*rushing into her embrace*) Mamma!

Picture.

CURTAIN.